Also by the Author

The Erin O'Reilly Mysteries
Black Velvet

Irish Car Bomb

White Russian

Double Scotch

Manhattan

Black Magic

Death by Chocolate

Massacre

Flashback

First Love

High Stakes

Aquarium (coming soon)

The Clarion Chronicles
Ember of Dreams

High Stakes

The Erin O'Reilly Mysteries
Book Eleven

Steven Henry

Clickworks Press • Baltimore, MD

First publication: Clickworks Press, 2021
Release: CP-EOR11-INT-H.IS-1.0

Sign up for updates, deals, and exclusive sneak peeks at clickworkspress.com/join.

Ebook ISBN: 978-1-943383-73-3
Paperback ISBN: 978-1-943383-74-0
Hardcover ISBN: 978-1-943383-75-7

For Dayton Police K-9 Rio, Anoka Police K-9 Bravo, Duluth Police K-9 Luna, and all the other real-life K-9s who are wounded or killed in the line of duty.

High Stakes

Stir 1 oz. each of vodka, mango rum, cherry brandy, orange juice, and pineapple juice together with 1 tbsp. Jägermeister herbal liqueur. Strain into a highball glass full of ice and serve.

Chapter 1

"Are you okay, kiddo?"

"I'm fine, Dad," Erin O'Reilly lied.

"We started down as soon as we heard," Sean O'Reilly said. He stood in the entryway of Erin's brother's brownstone, a house she could never have afforded. Her brother, Sean Junior, was a trauma surgeon at Bellevue Hospital and made something like four times her salary.

"I wanted to bring you a pie," Mary O'Reilly said, nudging her way around her husband's bulky frame. "But your father insisted on coming right away, so I didn't have time to bake."

"It's okay, Mom," Erin said. But she still felt the prickle of tears at the corners of her eyes when her mother gathered her into an embrace. "Seriously, I'm fine. The news blew this whole thing way out of proportion."

"I didn't hear it from the news," Sean said grimly.

"Sergeant Malcolm?" Erin guessed. The desk sergeant at Precinct 8 was an old friend of her dad's and had been known to pass him information from the department.

"Yeah." He looked her over. "I don't see any new holes."

"I didn't get hit," she said. "Didn't Malcolm tell you that?"

"You had a burglar in your apartment," Mary said, shaking her head sadly. "I don't know what this world's coming to."

"She wasn't a burglar, Mom," Erin said. "She was... never mind. The point is, I'm okay."

"That's good, dear," Mary said. "I'll let you and your father catch up on business." She bustled into the kitchen.

"Where's the rest of the family?" Sean asked.

"Anna and Patrick are in school," Erin said. "Junior's upstairs, asleep. He had a double shift in the ER that ran all last night. Michelle went to the store. And Rolf's watching my back."

Rolf, standing a little to one side of his partner, eyed Sean coolly. The German Shepherd's stare alone was enough to make hardened criminals back down.

"They won't let you go back home yet?" Sean asked.

"CSU finished going over the scene," Erin said. "So technically, I can sleep there if I want. I was able to drop by and get some of my things. But the living room carpet needs to be replaced. I've got a guy coming over at the end of the week. I don't think the... the stains are going to come out. Dad, we need to talk."

"Okay," Sean said. He set down his overnight bag beside his wife's suitcase. "Here?"

Erin shook her head. "Let's take a walk." She clipped Rolf's leash to his collar. Then she adjusted her Glock in its holster at her hip.

Her father noticed the motion. "Expecting trouble?" he asked.

"Ready for it," she replied.

"Mary!" Sean called. "We're going out for a few minutes."

"Don't be long, dear," she called back. "I just put the water on for some spaghetti."

Erin, her father, and Rolf, an active-duty detective, a retired

Patrol cop, and a K-9, set off along the sidewalk together.

"So what's the deal, kiddo?" Sean asked. "Malcolm told me it looked like a Mob hit on you. Is that what it was? Why don't you have a protection detail?"

"It's complicated, Dad," she said. She'd been dreading this conversation, but it had to happen now, before things got even further out of control. Her father had plenty of information sources in the NYPD, and he'd hear about it one way or another. That Siobhan Finneran, an assassin for the Irish Mob, had tried to kill her less than twenty-four hours ago wasn't the main point. Neither was the fact that Siobhan was now in the city morgue after Erin and Mob bodyguard Ian Thompson had gunned her down. The point was that Ian's boss, Morton Carlyle, was in the hospital after taking a bullet in the gut from Siobhan. Carlyle and Erin were lovers, had been for months. Sean knew Carlyle from his Patrol days and deeply distrusted him. But he'd learn about the two of them soon enough. Better he hear it now, from her.

The trouble was, there were things she wasn't allowed to tell him, and those were the very things that might make the situation bearable. Erin took a deep breath and tried to think how to explain.

"I've been seeing someone. For a while now. I wasn't sure how to tell you and Mom. Maybe I shouldn't have kept it a secret, but like I said, it's complicated."

Sean stopped and stared at her. Whatever he'd been expecting, it wasn't this. "You've been dating?" he asked. "That's your big secret?"

"Yeah."

"Well, that's great, kiddo. Mary's been worried about you, all alone here in the city. She's going to want to know why you've been sitting on it, sure, but she won't be mad. I guess I understand why you wouldn't want to tell her. She'd have the wedding halfway planned by now."

Erin shook her head. "That's not it, Dad. There's something I have to tell you. You have to promise you'll listen to me, okay? And not get mad."

"Mad?" Sean repeated. He rubbed his mustache. "Why would I get mad? You're a grown woman, Erin. I know things are different from when I was a kid. You can't think I'd go and get my shotgun just because... wait a second. Do you mean you're...?"

"Huh?" Erin was confused.

Sean glanced down at her stomach. "Well, I didn't think so, but I thought maybe you weren't, you know, showing yet..."

Erin followed his gaze. "Dad! I'm not pregnant!"

"You're not? Good. Great! I mean, it'd be great if you were, too, but only if you wanted to be. That is, I know Mary keeps going on about grandkids, and I'd be happy for you, too, only..."

"Dad. I'm not pregnant."

"Okay. Then I don't get the problem with this guy, why I'd get mad." Sean thought about it while Erin struggled to find the words. He snapped his fingers. "Is it? A guy, I mean? I know, it's the twenty-first century, and there's all this stuff going on... You know, Erin, I'm your dad. I'm going to love you no matter what. You can be seeing... you know, someone, and it doesn't matter if he's a she, you know?"

Erin gave a startled laugh. Just when she'd thought the conversation couldn't get any more awkward. "You think I'm a lesbian?"

"Well, if you were, I mean, I'd understand," Sean blustered.

It was sweet, in a weird, repressed way, Erin thought, watching her dad trying to come to terms with one theoretical revelation after another. And he would still love her, no matter what, which was a relief, she supposed. She wished it was that simple, that she'd found a nice girlfriend in Greenwich Village and was just awkward about coming out to her parents.

"I'm not," she said. "At least, I don't think so. It's a spectrum. Maybe I never met the right girl. No, it's a guy I've been seeing."

"Okay," Sean said, finally starting to work his old cop instincts. "This guy, you think I won't like him. Is he a cop? He's not that Russian guy you hang out with, is he?"

"Vic? No! My guy's not a cop. He's... Dad, he's Morton Carlyle."

Sean blinked. "Say what?"

"Morton Carlyle. Remember? From down in Queens, back in the day?"

"Carlyle... Cars Carlyle? Jesus, Erin, he's twice your age!"

"He's fifty, I'm thirty-five," she corrected him. "Fifteen years isn't double. Not even close."

"He's a gangster!"

This was where she had to be careful. Things were moving with Carlyle and the NYPD, things she'd been specifically ordered not to tell anyone, particularly family members or other cops. Sean was both.

"Dad, he's not as bad as you think. He treats me right. He doesn't kill people. He—"

"I can't believe you're this naïve!" Sean snapped. "Erin, he's a manipulator. He lies for a living. Maybe he doesn't get his hands dirty, but his people sure as hell do. He'll weasel his way in, make you trust him, but he doesn't care about you. These guys don't care about anyone but themselves!"

"Dad, he took a bullet for me. Last night."

"What are you talking about?"

"He was there. At my apartment. Siobhan, the woman with the gun, was about to shoot me. He went for her and she shot him. He's in the hospital right now, Dad. He nearly died trying to save me, so don't you dare tell me he doesn't care!"

Sean was taken aback. "I didn't mean that," he muttered

into his mustache.

"Yeah, you did," she said, not letting him get away with it. "You taught me the world has good guys and bad guys, and we're on the side of the good guys, but it's not always that simple. He's a good man, Dad. He just got in with some bad people."

"He's not some misguided teenager," Sean said. "He's a grown man. He knows what he's been doing. I'm going to ask around, find out what he's been up to. It might surprise you."

"Don't!" she said sharply.

"Erin, you have to know what this man's capable of."

"I do know," she said. "And I'm asking you, Dad. For my sake. Don't ask any of your old friends about him. And don't tell them anything. It could get him killed. It could get both of us killed. I... I think I can save him."

"You can't save people," he said. "Not if they won't let you."

Erin sighed. "I know. Look, let's go back to the house. Don't tell Mom about this, okay? She'll just worry."

"I don't like keeping secrets from your mother."

"How much crap happened to you on the Job without Mom ever hearing about it?"

"That's different."

"Yeah? How?"

"It just is, Erin! This is family, not business!"

"It's both." That was right up to the edge of what she could tell him. "Please, Dad, don't ask me any more about this. Not now. I promise, we'll sort this out one of these days, and it'll make sense then."

"I hope so. Because right now it makes no damn sense at all." Sean's mustache twitched in irritation. "Okay, you don't want to talk about this. Fine. You're the one who brought it up."

They walked in silence for a couple of minutes. Then Sean said, "You holding up okay otherwise?"

"Besides my boyfriend getting shot, and me getting in a gunfight in my living room? Yeah, I'm just peachy."

"We'll be hanging around for a few days. In case you need anything."

"Thanks, Dad."

"They got you on modified assignment? Because of the shooting?"

"Yeah."

"You miss working Patrol yet?"

"Sometimes. Is this the part where you tell me I shouldn't have taken that gold shield?"

"Hey, kiddo, when they tap you on the shoulder, you go where they tell you." Sean hesitated. "I'm proud of you, Erin. But I worry. And this Carlyle thing... It's a gamble. High stakes, a lot on the table."

"I'll be careful, Dad."

"Did being careful get you in a gunfight next to your coffee table?"

Erin smiled sadly. "Maybe not."

*   *   *

By the time they got back to the house, Mary O'Reilly was dishing out plates of steaming pasta. The smell wafting in from the kitchen suggested she'd also managed to indulge her baking impulse and had something in the oven. Some people showed love through gifts, some through sweet words, some through attention. Mary liked to show it through cooking. The only difficulty she didn't treat with food was an upset stomach, which helped explain Sean's expanding midsection.

"A phone call came for you, dear," Mary said to Erin as she set out plates for her and her dad. "It was a fellow who called himself Lieutenant Webb."

"What'd he want?" Erin asked.

"He said they've got some of your things at the station and you can pick them up whenever you'd like. They need to hold onto your revolver for a few days, but you can get your phone and some other items from Evidence. He said the investigation is closed."

"Great," Erin said. "I better go get my phone. People may need to get in touch with me."

"Right now, you need to sit down and get some good hot food in you," her mother corrected. "I don't know what you've been eating in this city, but you're way too thin. You need your nourishment. Here's a salad and some garlic bread. Store-bought, I'm afraid. I didn't have time to make meatballs or bake bread."

Erin resigned herself and sat. Rolf settled beside Anna's chair. He'd learned from previous visits that this was the best seat when it came to food mysteriously falling off the table. He was doomed to disappointment this time.

"Are you supposed to be at the station right now?" Sean asked.

"I'm on modified assignment, not vacation," she said. "Webb needs my paperwork on the incident, but I've been doing that here. I'm back on duty tomorrow. I expect then it'll be the same old grind. Internal Affairs already cleared me."

Sean blinked. "The OIS was less than twenty-four hours ago," he said, using the abbreviation for Officer-Involved Shooting in front of his wife the same way a parent might spell an unpleasant word so a toddler wouldn't get it. Erin suspected the fragile subterfuge wasn't getting anything past her mom.

"Yeah, they fast-tracked the review," she said.

"Still, it usually takes a few days," her dad said. "What do you know about your IA guy?"

"Enough to steer clear of him," she said, scowling at her

spaghetti. "Can we talk about something else, please?"

He let it go.

"I knew you might be in a hurry, dear," Mary said. "So I whipped up some chocolate-chip cookies. They'll be out of the oven in just a couple of minutes. You can take some of them to the station with you. Your father's colleagues always liked it when he brought in things I made."

"Thanks, Mom. It might take more than that to smooth my way." The sudden thought of Carlyle in a flowery apron, making food for the precinct, flitted through her head and she smothered a smile.

"Maybe," Mary said. "But cookies are always a good start. You know the way to a man's heart, don't you?"

"Through the stomach," Erin said. "Is that how you landed Dad?"

The two older O'Reillys looked at one another and smiled. "I always knew he was one of the good ones," Mary said. "So I set out to marry him, and I did. You'll know when you find the right one."

Sean and Erin tried not to react to that, deliberately avoiding eye contact with one another. Erin finished her hasty meal and stood up. Rolf bounced immediately to his feet, tail wagging, ready to go.

"Thanks, Mom," Erin said. "I'll see you later this evening."

"Wait, dear! Don't forget the cookies!" Mary bustled out to the kitchen.

Chapter 2

That was how Erin came into Precinct 8 with a Tupperware container full of fresh-baked cookies. She went downstairs to Evidence to get her stuff.

"Got something to check in?" the officer on duty behind the counter asked, looking hopefully at the container.

"Mom's cookies," she said. "Fresh baked. I'll trade you one for my phone."

"Police corruption is a terrible thing," he said, shaking his head. "You got a deal, Detective. Lieutenant Keane signed off on the file, so you're good to go. Let's see, we've got one Smartphone, light wear and tear. We had some bloodstains on it, looks like CSU dusted it for prints and got a match on your thumb off the case. We didn't clean it, sorry." He handed a plastic bag across the counter. It contained, as advertised, a beat-up, bloodstained phone coated with traces of fine fingerprint powder. "Just sign here."

Erin signed. "Anything else from my place?"

The officer checked his records. "Got a snub-nosed .38 special, five rounds chambered, one empty cartridge casing. We need to hold that. You got your duty piece on you?"

Erin patted the Glock at her hip. "Yeah, no problem."

"Good," he said. "We'll get this one back to you as soon as your bloodwork comes back."

"Forget about it," she said. It was standard practice after an officer was in a shooting to check the cop's system for drugs or alcohol. She'd been through it before.

"Okay," he said. "Then we're down to one television remote control, black in color, two AA batteries. And one beer glass, clear, clean. Both dusted for prints, the only prints matched to you. Sign here."

Erin did. She vaguely remembered those things as having been on her coffee table. Apparently CSU had bagged all the loose stuff around the shooting site. "I guess you've earned your cookie," she said, opening the container and handing one over.

"Still warm," he said and took an appreciative bite. "This is damn good, Detective. Tell your mom she's an angel."

"I'll pass that along, but I think she already knows," Erin said. She took the phone out of its baggie and looked at the bloody smear her hand had left on it. That was Carlyle's blood. She hadn't even noticed at the time. Shaking away the chill that ran down her spine, she pocketed the phone and stuck her TV remote in her other hip pocket. She didn't know what to do with the glass, so she just carried it in her hand.

On the way upstairs, she took a quick detour past the holding cells. They were empty. This wasn't unusual in the midafternoon. They'd fill up overnight, usually with drunk and disorderly idiots. A janitor was sweeping out one of them.

"Hey," she called to him. "You know what happened to Thompson, the guy they were holding?"

"Thin guy, buzz cut, tattoos on his arm?" the janitor asked. "Ex-military, I'd guess?"

"Yeah, that's him."

"You just missed him. Some fancy-pants lawyer turned him

loose a couple minutes ago. He might still be in the building."

Erin hurried upstairs. She'd wanted to talk to Ian Thompson. It wasn't just that he'd saved her life. She needed to sort out what he was going to say to Carlyle's boss.

She caught up with Ian and his lawyer at the front desk. The lawyer was signing something Sergeant Malcolm had given him. Ian was standing close to the wall, watching the room. He saw her at once and favored her with a polite nod.

"Hey, Ian," she said. "Got a second?"

The lawyer, whom Erin recognized as a guy named Walsh, smoothly stepped between them. He was a cold, professional man Evan O'Malley kept on retainer to handle his underlings' legal woes. "Detective, my client has been released from custody and will not be answering any questions. He's done nothing wrong."

"I know that, Walsh," she said. "I just need him for a second."

"Out of the question," Walsh said.

"Glad to, ma'am," Ian said simultaneously.

Walsh gave his client an irritated look. "Mr. Thompson, as your legal counsel—"

"It's not a problem, sir," Ian said.

"Let's step outside," Erin said. She didn't want to talk in front of other cops, or Walsh, for that matter. The lawyer, unfortunately, followed close on their heels, as if he had a leash like Rolf's. Rolf eyed Walsh warily.

Walsh had a car waiting outside the station, a black Lincoln Town Car. Caleb Carnahan, Carlyle's security chief, was leaning against its back door. The heavyset Irishman frowned when he saw Erin walking beside Ian.

"Go on and get in the car, sir," Ian said to Walsh. "I'll just be a moment."

"You shouldn't be talking to the cops," he said. "Especially not without a lawyer."

"Am I under arrest, ma'am?" Ian asked Erin.

"Of course not," she said.

"Then we're fine," Ian said to Walsh.

"That's not true," Walsh said.

"We're fine, sir," Ian repeated, and something in his eyes made Walsh turn and walk down the steps to the car.

"What is it, ma'am?" Ian asked, turning back to Erin.

She glanced at Walsh and Caleb, verifying they were out of earshot, and turned so they couldn't see her face. "I wanted to thank you," she said quietly.

"No thanks needed, ma'am. Just doing my job."

"You saved my life. And you saved Carlyle. He's going to make it."

He tried to hide it, but she saw the relief in his eyes. "Walsh said so," he said. "Wasn't sure whether to believe him."

"Ian, you're going to be talking to Evan O'Malley soon," she said. "Maybe Mickey Connor, too. You need to know what you're going to say to them."

"Was planning on the truth, ma'am."

"What if one of them sent Siobhan to my apartment?"

Ian's face froze. "You serious, ma'am?" His voice remained perfectly calm, but his eyes had turned sharp and hard as icicles.

"Someone in the O'Malleys sold me out to her," she said. "I don't know who. But it had to be someone who knew where we'd gone, and that I'd come back yesterday."

"Weren't many who knew," Ian said. "Carnahan and Quigley were on the plane. Mr. Carlyle and me. Maybe Corcoran and one or two others."

"I don't trust Caleb," she said. "Watch yourself, okay?"

He nodded infinitesimally. "Won't be a problem, ma'am. I'll take care of it."

"Thanks," she said. "Be careful."

"Affirmative. That all, ma'am?"

"I've told you before," she said, trying to smile. "It's Erin."

"Yes, ma'am." Then he turned and went down the stairs. Caleb opened the door of the Town Car and Ian climbed in. They drove away.

Erin watched the car disappear into the Manhattan traffic, then turned and went back inside the station. She went upstairs to the Major Crimes office, still carrying her mom's cookies in one hand, her beer glass in the other, Rolf's leash looped around her wrist.

Lieutenant Webb and Vic Neshenko were in the office. Webb glanced up when she came in. Vic didn't even look at her.

"I brought something my mom made," she said, holding up the Tupperware. "I'll just leave it in the break room."

"We can't take Mob kickbacks," Vic growled, still not looking up.

"You should still be home," Webb said.

"I'm cleared for duty, sir," she said.

He sighed. "I know, but you had a shooting incident yesterday. I've never heard of anyone getting cleared that fast, here or when I was with the LAPD. How'd you manage that?"

"I can guess," Vic muttered.

"That's enough, Neshenko," Webb said sharply.

"You got a problem with me, Vic?" Erin, never one to back down from a challenge, walked over to his desk. "Spit it out, before you choke on it."

Now he did look at her, and it took all Erin's inner grit and years of police experience not to take a step back. Vic was a big, muscular, rough-looking guy who loved a good fight. He was one of the toughest men she'd ever met, but she'd come to think of him as a friend. All she saw in his eyes was anger.

"You don't belong here," he said. "Shouldn't you be down at the Barley Corner? That's where you people hang out, isn't it?"

"I've never been dirty, Vic," she said. "And I'm not going to start now."

"I'm supposed to believe that? After you've been going behind our backs for months? Seeing a Mob guy?"

"Weren't you stepping out with a hooker who worked for the Russian Mafia last year?"

She hadn't really intended to say that. It just popped out.

"I didn't know she was a damn hooker!" Vic snarled, coming to his feet. "That was a setup! You knew goddamn well what he was! What'd he offer you? Money? Drugs? Or just the sex?"

Rolf bristled and growled. He didn't like anyone taking that tone with his partner.

"Screw you, Vic!" Erin snapped. "I've never taken drugs in my life, and I never took a cent off him!"

"No, just vacations and free drinks and favors," Vic sneered. He came around the desk, hands clenched. Rolf growled again, warningly.

"That's enough!" Webb shouted. "Both of you! Stand down!" He thrust himself between them, putting a hand on Vic's massive chest and another in Erin's face. He had about as much chance of pushing Vic backwards one-handed as he did of shoving Manhattan Island out into the North Atlantic, but Webb had enough angry authority in his voice that both his detectives paused.

"We're still professionals," Webb went on, after taking a calming breath. "Our job is to keep the peace, and I will not have fistfights breaking out right here in my own goddamned office." He turned to Vic. "Detective O'Reilly has been investigated by Internal Affairs and cleared of any wrongdoing. That is the official line, the only line. Do you understand?"

"Some investigation," Vic said under his breath. "It took her about two and a half minutes to sweet talk her way out of it. She probably just flashed her tits at the Captain and—"

Erin had heard plenty worse over her career on the streets, and it was such an absurd accusation it almost didn't make her angry. But the thought that Vic, who'd always had her back, might actually think that, let alone say it, hurt. She opened her mouth, not knowing what she was going to say.

Webb grabbed Vic by the collar with both hands, hooked a foot behind the other man's ankle, and slammed the big Russian back against his own desk. Taken completely off guard, Vic fell backward, sweeping a pile of DD-5 forms onto the floor.

"Have I got your attention, Neshenko?" Webb asked in a dangerously quiet voice. He was still holding Vic's collar, their faces about three inches apart.

"The hell is the matter with you, Lieutenant?" Vic sputtered.

"Good," Webb said, ignoring his answer. "I understand, some of this is my fault. I've put up with your insubordinate attitude because you're a damned good officer who gets good results. But this is it. You understand me? You don't go one step further, or I will sign your transfer papers myself. You'll go to Traffic Enforcement, or School Safety, or Housing Bureau, or whatever dipshit, small-time detail is willing to take you. If I ever hear you disrespect another officer who wears the shield, you are gone. Finished. Do you copy?"

"Jesus, sir," Erin said. "It's okay. Really."

"I'll get to you, O'Reilly. Wait your turn," Webb said, holding eye contact with Vic. "Do you copy, Neshenko?"

Vic nodded.

"Speak up," Webb said. "I never thought I'd live to see the day you'd hesitate to open your big mouth."

"Copy that, sir," Vic grated out.

Webb let go of him and stepped back. He took a moment to straighten his collar and necktie. Then he turned to face Erin.

"O'Reilly."

"Sir?" She didn't quite snap to attention, but she

straightened her back and tried to look professional. Webb was clearly in no mood to put up with bullshit.

"You understand the appearance your conduct may have created?"

"Yes, sir."

"We have thirty-five thousand officers in a city of over eight million," Webb said. "That means we're outnumbered by civilians more than two hundred to one. We don't maintain order by force. We do it by keeping up appearances. It's a bluff. When you damage the reputation of the New York Police Department, you put the entire system at risk. We have to be better than people expect us to be."

"Yes, sir."

"I have just one question for the two of you," he said, stepping back to look at them. "I can't be a babysitter or a couple's therapist. Can you work together, or not?"

Erin squared her shoulders. "I can, sir."

Vic's face twitched. "Sure, whatever," he muttered.

"That answer's not good enough for your mom, and it's sure as hell not good enough for me," Webb said.

"Yeah, I can," Vic said. "Sir."

"Good. Do I have to make you shake hands?"

"How about a group hug?" Erin suggested.

"Or we could make a circle, sing Kumbaya," Vic said. Neither of them cracked a smile, but the tension had gone down just a little. Maybe, Erin thought, it would be bearable. In time.

"All right," Webb said. "Now, what's in the box, O'Reilly?"

"Chocolate chip cookies. From my mom. Fresh."

"I'll have one," he said. "And you're going to eat one, Neshenko. That's an order. Are you done with your reports?"

"Not quite, sir," she said. "I'll have them for you by tomorrow morning."

"Good. We don't have any high-priority cases right now, so

why don't you go back home and finish writing up the incident report? Then you can turn it in when you come in tomorrow and we'll put this whole sorry mess behind us."

Erin understood that the subtext of Webb's request was to separate her and Vic while they cooled down. Accordingly, she took Rolf back out of the station without further protest. But she didn't go home. She went to Bellevue Hospital to check on her boyfriend. She'd leave Rolf in the car; it wouldn't be a long visit, and the day was cool enough he wouldn't overheat.

*   *   *

Two surprises were waiting for Erin at the hospital. The first was the police officer guarding Carlyle's room. He was an older, overweight officer who had probably been expecting a quiet assignment. Erin saw a chair, a coffee cup, and a copy of the New York Times next to the door. But the other surprise was in the process of making the officer's life difficult.

"I know who's in there, lad," James Corcoran was saying as Erin approached. "And we both know his name's not John bloody Doe. He's one of my mates. Are you telling me you're going to prevent me going through that door?"

"That's what I'm saying, punk," the officer said. To his credit, he was physically blocking the door with his considerable bulk.

"What's the problem, Corky?" Erin asked.

"Erin, love!" Corky exclaimed, turning to her with a sudden, brilliant smile spreading across his handsome, good-natured face. "You're the answer to my dreams and my prayers, rolled into one delightful bundle! I'm just explaining to this fine lad that I've come to visit my friend who's languishing in terrible pain, no doubt pining away with loneliness and despair."

"Corky," she said. "He's been there less than a day."

"Alone," he said, sadly shaking his head. "Just think of it."

"Who're you, ma'am?" the officer asked Erin. "This is a secure room. I'm gonna need to see some ID."

"O'Reilly, Major Crimes," she said, showing her shield.

"Oh," he said, glancing at the gold detective shield and becoming more respectful. "Sorry, ma'am. Orders. You know this guy?"

"Yeah," she said. "Don't worry, I'll take care of him."

"Grand," Corky said cheerfully. "You've no notion how long I've waited to hear you say those words."

"That's not what I meant," she said. She took his arm and pulled him a short distance down the hall, away from the officer. "What the hell are you doing here?"

"I've just told you," he said. "I've come to see my mate."

"I mean, how did you know he was here?"

"New York's ambulance drivers are affiliated with the Teamsters," he said.

That was all the explanation Erin needed. Corky was Carlyle's best friend, a middle management associate in the O'Malleys. His responsibility, as she understood it, was to make and maintain contacts with New York's transportation network. Organized crime involved a great deal of smuggling, together with shady construction contracts, garbage collection, and shipping rackets. Corky was the man who could get what you needed where you needed it. He was close with a lot of union officials, particularly in the Teamsters.

"I thought you were in Mexico," she said.

"I was, until I heard. Then I caught the first flight back. It's true, is it? Cars caught one? How bad is he hurt?" Corky was still smiling, but he looked concerned.

Erin studied his face. She'd always liked Corky, had even briefly dated him before she really knew what he got up to, but could she trust him? As she'd told Ian, someone had sold them out, and Corky was one of the few who'd known their plans.

"Bad enough," she said at length. "But he's going to pull through."

"Ah, that's grand," he said with what appeared to be genuine relief. "I'd heard he took one in the belly?"

"Yeah."

"That's a rough break, love. But there's worse places a man can be shot." He winked. "Have you got the bastard who did it?"

"Yeah," she said again. "The shooter's dead."

Corky nodded. "There's something to be glad for. Who was it?"

"I really can't discuss it."

"Erin. It's me!"

"Is that supposed to encourage me?"

He laughed. "Can you get me past the guard at the door?"

"We'd better not," she said. "But you'll need to talk to Carlyle soon. I'll set something up. I promise." One of the conditions Carlyle had set for his cooperation with the police was that Corky be brought into the operation, but Erin wasn't prepared to do that right this minute. They needed to handle this very carefully.

"Your word's good with me," Corky said, grinning again. "And if you're needing any comfort in this difficult time, I'll clear my schedule for you, day or night."

"I'll bet you will."

"One question only, love."

"Only one?"

"Was it one of ours?"

"Was what?"

"The hit."

Corky's use of the word "ours" rocked Erin back on her heels. She stared at him. What did he mean? He might be talking about their shared ethnic background, but she didn't think so.

He'd started thinking of her as being one of his people. Someone in what criminals called "the Life." That made sense, she supposed. Vic had come to the same conclusion. How was it possible to become a criminal without actually committing any crimes?

"You know I can't tell you that," she said.

He nodded. "I'll just have to follow my own instincts, then. Take care, love. And keep an eye over your shoulder. I'm thinking these won't be the only bullets aimed at us."

There it was again. "Us." Erin suppressed a shudder as she watched him walk away. Then she went back to Carlyle's room.

The guard let her in, but she could tell he was watching her through the window in the door to make sure nothing untoward happened. Erin wished just one person would trust her, on either side of the law. That would make a nice change.

"Hello, darling," Carlyle said quietly.

"Hey. How're you feeling?" She approached the bed. He looked better than he had that morning. His color was better, probably because of all the blood they'd been pumping in to refill his veins.

"I'm well, considering. Did I hear Corky's voice out there?"

"Yeah. But the guard wouldn't let him in."

He smiled thinly. "I can't say I blame him."

"But Corky's your best friend!"

Carlyle's smile faded. "Aye. In the Life, your best friend is the lad they send to kill you."

"You can't mean that. About him."

He shook his head. "Nay, darling, it's the truth. Why do you think Corky's so important to me? He's the one lad in the O'Malleys I don't think would kill me. But then, that's what Evan would want me to think. If Evan wants me dead, he'd likely tell Corky to do it. Or Siobhan, come to that."

Erin sucked in a breath. "You think Evan's the one who

tried to have you killed?"

"It's possible."

Erin thought it over. "Either he or one of his guys set it up," she agreed. "But that doesn't mean he necessarily knew about it. It could've been someone farther down the chain."

"Has Evan contacted you?" Carlyle asked, trying to force himself to a more upright position. His stitched-together abdominal muscles wouldn't allow it. He sagged back. "Damnation. I can't do a bloody thing lying here."

"I haven't heard from him," Erin said. "But he sent Walsh to get Ian out of lockup. Walsh and Caleb took Ian to see Evan, I think."

Carlyle nodded. "That's promising, so far as it goes."

"Why?"

"It suggests Evan's trying to find out what happened."

"Why is that good?"

"Because if he doesn't know, it means he likely wasn't behind it."

"Okay," Erin said. "Who knew we were flying back from the Bahamas? They had to know the schedule, and where we'd been."

"You and me, naturally," Carlyle said. "Evan almost certainly. Ian, Caleb, and Quigley. Perhaps Mickey. Any one of them may have told others."

"Ian wouldn't have," Erin said. "Ian had the same list as you. Plus Corky."

"It wasn't Corky," Carlyle insisted. "Nor Ian. Ian's got a good head on his shoulders, and he's fond of what he'd call operational security. Not a talkative lad, our Ian. Besides, if he'd wanted us dead, we'd be both of us dead. He'd have done it himself."

Erin nodded. "That leaves Caleb, Quigley, and maybe Mickey. I don't know Quigley."

"He's one of my lads," Carlyle said. "He's always been solid."

"How long has he been with you?"

"Eight, ten years."

"What about Caleb?"

"He's been running security at the Corner for years."

"Is he one of your guys, too? Someone you recruited?"

"Nay. He came from Evan."

"You trust someone you didn't pick to handle your security?"

Carlyle's smile was cynical. "You're assuming I'd some choice in the matter. A great deal of Evan's money moves through the Corner. He'd be the one to pick the lad who's minding the door."

"I don't trust Caleb," she said for the second time that day.

"I'd trust him to protect me as long as it's what Evan wants," Carlyle said. "But if there's a difference of opinion in the O'Malleys, it's not necessarily my side he'd be taking."

"One of them has to be involved," she said. "Caleb and Quigley were the pilot and copilot. They set the schedule. What can we do about it?"

"Do?" Carlyle looked surprised. "Right now there's little enough I can do. But I'd think you'd know by now how this sort of thing gets handled in the Life."

She swallowed. "Right. But how can you be sure you're aiming at the right target?"

"My folk don't need to be sure," he said softly. "That's a policeman's prerogative. Suspicion's enough to go on. Speaking of which, how are your people handling matters? Are they treating you well?"

"Vic's pissed off. So is Webb, I think."

"They're thinking you've betrayed them?"

She sighed. "Pretty much."

"They'll have to go on thinking that," he said. "And you have to accept it. That's part of this devil's bargain we've made. Both of us have to accustom ourselves to people thinking we're something we're not. It'll all come out in the end, but till then, it's a rough road we're traveling. You can still walk away. Perhaps you should."

She took his hand. "I'm not leaving you now," she said. "When you're lying in a hospital bed with a hole in your gut because of me? Jesus. What kind of girlfriend would I be?"

"The sensible kind," he said, but he smiled as he said it and squeezed her hand. Then his face twisted in sudden pain. "Darling, there's a wee box to my right. Could you reach it for me?"

She found it, a button attached to a cord, and handed it to him. He immediately pushed it three times. Erin knew it was the control for his morphine drip. He was in more pain than he would ever let on.

"Are you okay?" she asked, already knowing the answer.

"I'll live," he said through tight-clenched teeth. "You'd best be on your way, darling. I'll be grand."

"There's an NYPD guy at the door," she said. "You'll be safe."

He nodded. "Be careful, darling."

She gave his hand a squeeze, not daring any more obvious show of affection with the guard watching. Then she stood up, went to the door, and opened it.

"Nobody goes in who isn't on the hospital's medical staff," she told the officer. "I mean it, nobody. And check the credentials of any nurse or doctor."

"Copy," the cop said. "Who is this guy, anyway?"

"You're better off not knowing," she said.

Chapter 3

Erin started driving back to her brother's house in Midtown, but she was only about halfway when her phone buzzed with an unidentified number. That usually meant either Carlyle or a scam, and she knew Carlyle didn't have access to a phone. She almost let it ring, but a cop wasn't supposed to do that.

"O'Reilly," she said.

"You have a meeting with our guy. Can you get to Hell's Kitchen Park in half an hour?"

"Who is this?" Erin demanded. The voice was familiar but she couldn't immediately place it over the phone.

"Is this a secure line?" The voice turned slightly mocking.

That did the trick for her. *Keane, you son of a bitch,* she thought. "I think you'd know that better than I would, Lieutenant," she said.

Lieutenant Keane laughed softly. "Indeed I would. You're looking for a man wearing eyeglasses. He'll be sitting on a bench, by himself, doing the Times crossword."

"This guy got a name?"

"He'll tell you everything you need to know. Welcome to undercover work, Detective." Keane hung up.

"Bastard," Erin muttered. She glanced over her shoulder, reassuring herself with Rolf's quiet, intense presence. "You'd never rat me out to Internal Affairs, would you, partner?"

Rolf opened his mouth and let his tongue hang out over his teeth.

"Yeah, you're smiling now," she said. "This bullshit stops being funny when it starts being you."

She was partway to Hell's Kitchen already, since it lay right next to Midtown. It was traditionally the home of lower-class Irish in Manhattan, but Erin didn't know it well. The neighborhood had been heavily gentrified in the '90s, housing prices rising to compete with its posh neighbors. Erin found the park easily enough with the aid of her onboard computer. She parked the Charger in a police spot and unloaded Rolf. They walked into the park together, Erin scanning the area for anyone fitting Keane's description, Rolf sniffing the air.

Growing up on a diet of Hollywood movies, she was expecting a shady-looking guy in a trench coat and fedora, or maybe a tough-looking Special Forces type with tattoos and scars. What she saw was a mild-looking man who looked to be in his mid-forties. He didn't look like a spy; he didn't even look like a cop. He was losing a battle with his waistline, which filled out a button-down shirt and blue blazer. He was clean-shaven and going bald. If he was wearing a gun, she didn't see one. But he was wearing eyeglasses and holding a ball-point pen in one hand, a copy of the Times in the other, and sitting on a park bench.

Erin walked slowly up to him, looking around for any backup or surveillance. She saw nothing out of the ordinary, but then, she'd have walked right by this guy on the street and assumed he was a civilian. He looked like he ought to be teaching high school civics, not waiting on a clandestine meeting with a detective.

He looked up from his paper, as if sensing her approach. Erin was a good judge of eyes and body language. His eyes were soft and thoughtful, his posture nonthreatening. He folded the paper and set it down on the seat beside him. He stood up and his eyes traveled quickly around the park. He was checking the same things she had.

"Detective O'Reilly, I presume?" he said.

"Yeah," she said. "I was told I had a meeting with you."

He smiled. "Thanks for making the time." He held out his hand. "Phil Stachowski. I'm a lieutenant at Precinct 10, but don't bother with the protocol. I work with undercovers and informants, so I tend to be a little more informal than some. You can just call me Phil."

"Glad to meet you," Erin said, taking the offered hand. He had a good grip, firm and steady. "Erin O'Reilly. This is Rolf."

"I've heard a lot about you," Phil said. "Can I call you Erin, or would you prefer O'Reilly?"

"Whichever," Erin said, managing to swallow the automatic "sir" she nearly put on the end. She was used to having a little latitude with her own lieutenant, but she knew Webb. Lieutenant Stachowski was a mystery to her and her training was threatening to take over.

"Erin, then," he said. "Have a seat. It sounds like we've got some things to talk about."

"Can I see some ID?" she asked. "Nothing personal, but this whole thing is kind of iffy, and I don't want to go off the rails any more than I have to."

He was still smiling. "Certainly, Erin. I see you already understand one of the primary principles of undercover work."

"What's that?"

"Everything's a test, all the time," he said. He flipped open his wallet and showed her what did, indeed, appear to be an NYPD Lieutenant's shield next to a driver's license that matched the name he'd given. "They're going to test you at every turn, sometimes deliberately, sometimes by accident. And unfortunately, you can pass ninety-nine times out of a hundred and that last one can trip you up. Have you done undercover work before?"

"Not really," she said, seating herself on the other end of the bench. Rolf settled on his haunches next to her, eyeballing Phil. The Shepherd hadn't made up his mind about this whole thing.

"I've read the O'Malley files," Phil said. "Captain Holliday sent them over to me last night. As I understand it, you've formed a personal connection with Morton Carlyle?"

Erin felt her jaw clench, but forced herself to relax. She'd have to get used to her personal life being discussed in tactical terms. That was part of the deal. "That's right," she said.

He nodded, and she realized that had been her first test. She wondered whether she'd passed.

"This Carlyle seems like a solid source in the O'Malleys," he went on. "He's an associate in good standing and it appears he's one of the men in line to succeed Evan O'Malley. How did you get to know him?"

"I investigated him as a murder suspect last year," she said.

Phil's laugh was very pleasant, very natural. "Not a very promising start to a relationship," he said.

Erin smiled. "I saved his life and his place of business. He figured he owed me one. We started a business relationship, trading information and small favors."

Phil listened as Erin laid out the framework of how she and Carlyle had gradually come to trust one another. She described all the cases he'd helped with, the dangers they'd faced, the fights they'd been through side by side. When she was done, he leaned back and whistled softly.

"Holliday told me this was a little unusual," he said. "Normally, when we send someone to infiltrate an organized-crime racket, the whole point is that the target doesn't know our guy is a cop. But in this case, you're already known as a decorated detective. That brings both good and bad news with it."

"What's the bad news?" she asked, taking her cue.

"They know you carry a shield. They don't trust you."

"And the good news?"

"The operation can't be blown by them finding out you're a cop," he said with a grin. "You don't have to disguise *what* you are, only *who* you are. It's a difficult dance."

"How do you mean?" Erin asked.

Phil leaned forward. His eyes were dark brown, and as he looked at her, Erin saw that under the surface softness he had an intensity to him. "A lot of undercover officers think the worst danger is they'll get found out and someone will shoot them. And you do need to be careful about that, but you're obviously an experienced and sensible officer, so I won't insult you by harping on that point. The worst danger for you, Erin, is you can get lost in the role. You can forget who you are and what you're trying to do."

"The hell of this job is, you need to make friends with people, get them to like you, even love you, while planning to destroy them. If you do your job right, when we put the cuffs on them and put them in interrogation rooms they won't give up your name because they'll still think you're on their side. They'll want to protect you. You need to earn their loyalty and betray them. Not everybody can do that. Can you?"

"I think so, yeah," Erin said, with one inner reservation. She wasn't going to betray Carlyle.

Phil's posture relaxed slightly. "Good. Hey, Erin, it's going to be okay. This is serious, we both know that, but I've run plenty of undercover ops before. I'm going to be your liaison. This is Captain Holliday's operation, but you're not to go to him with anything unless it's an absolute emergency and you can't reach me."

"Yeah, Keane told me that," Erin said.

"And you don't go to Keane with anything," Phil said. "Not unless Holliday and I are both out of the picture."

"Why not? Because he's Internal Affairs?"

"Because I know Andrew Keane," Phil said. "He's a politician. He's ambitious and inherently untrustworthy. The more people who know what you're doing, the more chance there is of this going sideways. Ideally, I want this to be you, me, and your contact. Here's a phone."

He slid an old-school cheap flip-phone along the bench toward her.

"I'm programmed in, my contact listed as Leo."

"Nickname?" Erin guessed.

"Sign of the Zodiac," he said with a smile. "You can call me anytime, for any reason. I'll answer if I can. If I can't, don't leave a message unless it's absolutely essential. I'll return your call within half an hour. I'll be drawing up a plan of action for us. As long as Carlyle is cooperative, it should be pretty straightforward. He'll be doing all the heavy lifting."

"There's a wrinkle," Erin said. "He's in the hospital right now."

"So I hear," Phil said, nodding. "That's no worry. We're in no particular rush. You never want to rush an undercover op. When people rush is when they make mistakes. For now, I just needed to meet you, talk to you face-to-face, make sure you're up for this."

"If I'm up for this?" she repeated, raising an eyebrow.

"Exactly," he agreed. "I think we'll work well together, Erin. I'll be in touch. Keep this phone near you, charged, and turned on. If you don't answer, I'll assume you're okay. I won't leave messages, nothing that would compromise you. You're on the sharp end on this; there's no emergency on my end that's ever going to justify risking your cover."

He stood up. "Glad we've had this talk. Do you have any questions for me?"

Erin had so many she didn't even know what to say. But one of them floated to the top of her consciousness. "Does this sort of thing work? I mean, are we going to be able to pull this off?"

"It usually goes okay," he said. "Just keep your mind on what you're doing. And remember who you are."

"I never forget," she said.

* * *

Erin finally got back to the O'Reilly house, just in time for dinner. She smelled the food as soon as she opened the door; Mary had obviously spent the afternoon making her famous pot roast. Erin glanced down at her partner and smiled. Rolf was too proud to beg, but the Shepherd's body was betraying him. A thin strand of drool was already working its way from his jowl toward the floor.

The whole O'Reilly clan had assembled. Erin's three brothers were all there: Sean Junior, Michael, and Tommy. Michael's wife Sarah was talking with Michelle, while Anna and Patrick played some sort of game on the living room floor involving a wooden train set and a small herd of pastel-colored toy horses. Tommy had his guitar out and was meditatively picking out a melody. Erin's dad, in the middle of it all, was placidly reading the Times. Michael, next to him, had appropriated the Business section of the paper.

Mary came bustling out of the kitchen. "We're just about ready," she said. "Oh, Erin! There you are, dear!"

"Rolfie!" Anna shouted and charged toward Rolf with her arms wide. The K-9 had faced down armed felons. He'd been shot, Tased, and beat up. He didn't flinch from the little girl's squealing onslaught, merely giving Erin a look of long-suffering patience as Anna wrapped her arms around his neck.

"Gang's all here," Erin said.

"It isn't often we all get together," Michelle said. "Sorry. I should've warned you."

"It's okay," Erin said. "Hey, family are the people you can't get rid of, right?"

"Depends," Tommy said. "I bet you know a guy, right, Sis? Know any good hitmen?"

Erin's dad slowly lowered his paper and gave her a meaningful look.

She pretended not to see it. "If I do, Tommy, you'll be the first one I'm sending them after."

"Tommy O'Reilly sleeps with the fishes," he said, doing his best Godfather impression, which wasn't a very good one.

Dinner was a raucous affair. Erin let the rest of her family carry the conversation. She had a lot on her mind. Phil Stachowski seemed like a nice guy, but a nice guy wasn't what Erin needed. She needed someone competent, someone who would have her back. At least he wasn't pissed off at her like the entire rest of the NYPD. And then there were the Irish to consider. What had Ian told Evan O'Malley? What would Evan do? Would he hold her responsible for what had happened to Carlyle? Or had it been his plan all along, to kill both of them?

"You need to keep up your strength, dear," Mary said.

"Huh?" Erin hadn't been paying any attention.

"You're just pushing your food around your plate. Did I mess something up? I thought pot roast was one of your favorites."

"It is. Sorry. It's just..." Erin didn't know how to finish the sentence.

"Don't badger her, Mary," her dad said quietly. "She's had a rough time."

"Of course," Mary said. "I just thought some comfort food might do some good."

Erin saw tears in her mother's eyes and felt suddenly bad for her. Mary was trying to help the best way she knew, and she didn't know the whole story. Erin forced herself to concentrate on the taste of the food, the way it warmed her on the way down. After a while, she really did feel a little better.

After dinner, Anna and Patrick played with Rolf for a while, before Michelle hauled them up to bed despite their sleepy protests. The adults talked and drank coffee. Erin heard some of Sean Junior's funny medical stories, some of Michael's boring business stories, and some of Tommy's bizarre musician stories. She and her dad contributed a few police anecdotes. It was a pleasant enough evening that she was able to almost forget all the crazy chaos waiting for her.

About ten thirty, the other O'Reilly siblings said their goodbyes, exchanged hugs, and left for their own homes; Michael and Sarah's swanky downtown apartment and Tommy's Greenwich Village loft which he shared with three to five other musical types, depending on the state of their finances.

"Did you smell reefer on Tommy?" Sean quietly said in Erin's ear.

"Yeah. You want to talk to him about it?"

He shook his head. "No point. That kid's gonna do what he does. I just wish he'd get a real job."

"You mean, a job where you get shot at?" Erin joked.

"I mean a job that pays actual money. Guitar won't get you anywhere. For every Elvis, there's a thousand guys playing on street corners for spare change."

"Dad, do you ever stop worrying about your kids? We're grown up now."

"Never. You'll find that out if you ever have kids of your own." He sighed. "Little pieces of your heart running around, making bad choices, getting in trouble. And you wonder why I've got such a big gun cabinet."

"You can't shoot everything that comes after us, Dad."

"A man can dream." He put an arm around her shoulders. "I even worry about you, kiddo, and you're the toughest of the bunch. I guess a girl with nothing but brothers is either going to grow up safe and sheltered, or tough as nails."

"If I have to choose, I'll take the nails," she said, putting an arm around her dad in return.

"That's my girl."

Erin's phone buzzed. She fished it out and saw Webb's name. "Great," she muttered, then hit the answer icon on the screen. "O'Reilly."

"Got that paperwork done yet?" Webb asked.

"I'll have it for you tomorrow, sir," Erin said. "Like I promised."

"Not if you're not done yet," he said.

"What do you mean?"

"You're back on the clock. We just caught a body. Not too far from your place, actually." He gave the address.

Erin's heart skipped a beat. "That's right next to..."

"The Barley Corner, yeah," Webb said. "The alley behind it. Go on and get to the scene. You'll probably be there before we are. Neshenko's got a bit of a drive."

"I'm not at home," she said. "I'm at my brother's, in Midtown. But I can be there in twenty."

"Copy," Webb said. "See you there."

"Work?" Sean asked as she hung up.

"Yeah. Back to work."

"You okay, kiddo?"

"Always."

* * *

It might be a coincidence, Erin told herself. The Corner had a lot of Mob activity around it. Maybe it had nothing to do with Carlyle's shooting. Maybe it wasn't even a homicide. People dropped dead on New York streets all the time. Heart attacks, seizures, car accidents.

She kept repeating comforting theories to herself all the way there. At least it couldn't be Carlyle himself. He was in a hospital bed under police guard. Besides, he didn't hang out behind the pub. The back door of the Corner was steel core and protected by a state-of-the-art security system. It had nothing to do with him.

She parked the Charger alongside the other police vehicles already on scene. She didn't see an ambulance. Either the EMTs had come and gone, or the state of the body had made it obvious their services wouldn't be required. She unloaded Rolf and headed for the alley, flashing her shield to a couple of Patrol officers standing guard at the entrance.

The smell hit her right away. It was like copper, almost, but with an organic undertone. The scent of blood was impossible to mistake for anything else. She also caught a faint whiff of gunpowder. That meant the scene was fresh, certainly less than an hour old. Up ahead, she saw a couple more uniforms standing with their flashlights trained on the body. It was behind a dumpster. She could see the feet sticking out, clad in brown leather shoes and jeans.

"What've we got here?" she called to the officers.

"Single victim," the sergeant in charge of the scene said. "White male. Two GSW, one in the hand, one right through the forehead. Exit wound damn near took off the back of his head."

"Ouch," Erin said. She walked around the dumpster, keeping Rolf on a short lead. The Shepherd sniffed at the man's foot and went into his alert posture, indicating the presence of a dead body. Erin's gaze traveled up the corpse, starting at the feet. Nice shoes, not overly fancy. Fairly new jeans. A white button-down shirt, dirty and stained with blood and alley debris. The man was heavyset, with a big gut. His right hand was covered with blood, a pool of it soaking into his pants. He'd taken a bullet there for sure. He had a gold necklace with some sort of Celtic charm on it. Finally, Erin let her eyes rest on the dead man's face.

The bottom dropped out of her stomach. "Shit," she whispered.

"Yeah," one of the other cops agreed. "Not a nice way to go. At least it was quick."

Erin hoped the flashlights wouldn't show how pale her face probably was. She thought she might throw up. It wasn't the fact of the body, or the way the man had died.

"We haven't ID'd him yet," the sergeant said. "If it was a robbery, he won't have his wallet. But maybe facial recognition..."

She shook her head. They wouldn't need facial recognition. She knew the dead man. And his death meant all kinds of trouble.

Caleb Carnahan, Carlyle's chief of security, lay dead behind the building it had been his job to protect. His eyes, wide open and staring, showed a last instant of shocked disbelief. A splatter of blood was sprayed across the brickwork behind his head like a ghastly halo.

Chapter 4

Erin stared at Caleb's body. One thought kept running through her head, something she'd said, the answer she'd gotten.

"I don't trust Caleb. Watch yourself, okay?"

"Won't be a problem, ma'am. I'll take care of it."

Had she taken out a contract on a man, without even meaning to? Mob guys were careful about not telling their people explicitly to kill other guys. It was just understood. But surely Ian wouldn't have taken it that way. He knew she wasn't a mobster.

Except that she *was* a mobster. At least, that was what everyone was supposed to think. Erin pressed a hand against her forehead. This was enough to drive a person crazy.

The uniformed officers had moved off to the entrance to the alley, giving her some space. Now that a detective was on scene, their job was to preserve the scene and guard the perimeter. Erin ignored them and kept trying to think.

"What the hell are you doing here?"

She didn't bother to turn. "Got the call, same as you, Vic."

"Just like that, you're back on the squad?"

"I never left the squad."

"Maybe you should."

"Maybe you should kiss my ass."

"No thanks. I don't wanna touch anything that mope's had his hands all over."

Now she did turn to face him. "Okay, you know what? Screw you, Vic. How much of this is because I'm a woman?"

"The hell you talking about?" he snapped. "That's got nothing to do with this!"

"Doesn't it? What if I was a guy who'd stepped out with some mob chick? Then it'd just be 'Boys will be boys,' and nobody would give a damn. But a woman sleeps with a guy, all of a sudden she's a slut, is that it?"

"I never called you that."

"You're thinking it. It's all over your face."

Vic's jaw clenched. "Don't you dare," he said in a dangerously quiet voice. "This isn't about me. I didn't do a damn thing wrong here. You could've screwed up any number of cases. You could get convicted perps sprung. That's what happens when there's misconduct."

"There wasn't any misconduct," she shot back. "IAB says so."

"I'm supposed to believe that? Why did IAB clear you so quick, Erin? What'd you say to Keane? What'd he say to you?"

She shook her head. "I can't tell you that, Vic." She tried to soften her voice. "I'm sorry."

"Sorry? You're sorry? Well that's just great, then. Everything's fine, 'cause you're sorry. Jesus."

"You told Webb we could work together," she reminded him. "You want to go to work, or what?"

"I didn't sign up for this bullshit," he muttered. "Look, Erin, I trusted you. I had your back. Every damn time!"

"I know. And I feel like crap for how this all got sprung on you. Look, I didn't mean for any of this to happen. One thing just sort of led to another, and here we are."

"You had choices. Every step of the way. And you knew this wasn't right, or you wouldn't have kept it a secret."

Erin took a breath. "You know what, Vic? Maybe you're right. Maybe this was the wrong thing for me to do, and the wrong way to do it. But I'm doing things right from here on out, okay? I'm trying here."

"I just hope nobody gets killed because of it," he grumbled. "So who's the stiff?"

Erin sighed. "His name's Caleb Carnahan."

Vic blinked. "You know this guy? Well, yeah, I guess maybe you would. You hang out at this bar a lot. Who is he? A regular?"

"He ran security at the Corner."

Vic stared at her. His mouth hung open. "Shit. He's one of Carlyle's guys?"

Erin nodded.

"Are we supposed to think this is a coincidence?" Vic went on.

"I'm pretty sure it isn't."

"So a guy is dead because of you."

"We don't know that," she said. "Someone could be moving on the O'Malleys. Or it could be something internal. I hardly knew Caleb."

Lieutenant Webb stepped into the alley. "Oh, good. Both of you are here," he said. "Sorry I'm a little late. What'd I miss?"

Vic looked at Erin.

"It's a homicide," she said. "Caleb Carnahan. Shot twice, once in the hand, once in the head."

"You sure on the ID?" Webb asked.

"I've met the guy a couple of times," she confirmed.

"Known associates?" he asked.

"He's one of Evan O'Malley's guys. Handled security for the Barley Corner."

Webb put a hand over his face. "Fantastic," he muttered. "Okay, you know what, O'Reilly? You cannot take lead on this investigation."

"Why not, sir?"

Webb and Vic gave her identical looks.

"You going to make me explain, O'Reilly?" Webb asked.

Erin shook her head. "No, sir. I get it." She was internally raging at the unfairness of it. But then she thought about Ian again, and their conversation, and wondered if she should be within a mile of this case.

Webb moved past her and looked down at Caleb's body. "Doesn't look like he was dumped here," he said. "Check out the blood on the wall."

"Yeah," Vic said. "That's from the exit wound. He was shot right here. And he was already on the ground, see?"

"Otherwise the spatter would be higher up," Erin agreed, trying to forget her internal conflict by focusing on the clues in front of her. "Where's Levine?"

"She's on the way," Webb said. "Any minute now."

Sarah Levine was the Medical Examiner for Precinct 8, an odd but extremely competent woman. There was no one better at determining what had happened to human remains.

"I noticed the smell of gunpowder when I got here," Erin said. "This happened recently."

"Blood's still wet," Vic confirmed, shining his flashlight on the wall. "If it didn't ricochet, the bullet's gonna be somewhere in this brickwork. Hey, I got the bullet hole here." He pointed to a brick. Sure enough, his flashlight beam reflected off something metallic lodged in the wall.

"That's one of them," Webb said. "But looks like he was shot twice. Going through his hand, that bullet could be anywhere."

"No footprints or fingerprints," Erin said. The alley was asphalt. She played her own light along the ground. "Cartridge case! There!"

Webb followed her pointing finger. A small, hollow piece of brass lay next to the dumpster. The Lieutenant knelt beside it and put down a yellow plastic marker for the CSU guys to see. Erin joined him, ducked her head, and sniffed at the casing. It still smelled smoky.

"I think this is it," she said. "It's fresh, at any rate."

"I don't see a gun on our dead guy," Vic said. He snorted. "Some security man. He's got a holster on him, but no piece."

"So the killer took it," Webb said. "Either before he was killed, or maybe afterward. If the other guy got the drop on him, he may not have had a chance to draw. Suppose the first bullet was the one that caught him in the hand."

"Yeah," Vic said. "Looks like it went right through the middle of the palm. That happens to a guy, he's not holding anything with those fingers. It would've taken out half the tendons on the way through." He paused. "Of course, if the first bullet was the one that blew his brains out, I don't think he'd have pulled a gun then, either."

Erin was only half listening. She directed Rolf's snout toward the cartridge casing. The Shepherd sniffed at it curiously and adopted the position alerting his partner to the presence of explosives.

"*Such,*" she said to Rolf in his native German, his "seek" command. She was hoping the gunman had handled the bullet with a bare hand. If he had, they might or might not get a usable fingerprint from the casing, but the shooter would have left some skin cells on the ammunition regardless. That could be enough for Rolf to track him.

The Shepherd moved his head from side to side, trying to pick up the scent. Erin had heard a dog's nose was so sensitive that they could tell the direction of a smell depending on which nostril it entered first. Then the K-9 started moving, tail wagging.

"What's the point of that?" Vic wondered aloud. "The guy had a car waiting for sure. He's long gone, Erin."

But Rolf didn't go all the way out of the alley. He stopped at the dumpster. Then he stood up on his hind legs, planted his front paws on the lip of the metal bin, and snuffled at the lid. He whined.

"Something's in there," Erin said. She drew her sidearm and moved to the far corner of the dumpster.

"Our shooter's still here?" Vic wondered aloud. "Easiest case I've ever seen." He drew his Sig-Sauer automatic and went to the other corner of the bin. "Ready."

Webb stepped in and took hold of the lid. He flipped it open and stepped back. Vic and Erin moved in, guns and flashlights trained.

All they saw was a heap of black plastic trash bags.

"Clear," Vic said disappointedly. "Nobody's inside."

"Rolf smelled something," Erin insisted. "We have to take a look."

"Okay, O'Reilly," Webb said. "Take a look."

Erin saw a smug look on Vic's face, but couldn't argue the logic. Being a detective sometimes meant dumpster-diving for evidence. She pulled on a pair of disposable gloves. "*Bleib*," she ordered Rolf, telling him to stay put. Then she levered herself up and into the trash bin.

It wasn't the most disgusting thing she'd ever had to stand in. She'd once slogged her way through the sewers under

Manhattan. That had been much worse. But the smell of half-rotten food nauseated her as she began probing through the garbage bags. She wondered how Rolf could make out a particular scent.

"If you're wrong about this," she told her dog, "I'm going to kick your furry ass."

Rolf, sitting obediently where she'd left him, seemed confident.

Then, in a corner of the bin, Erin saw it. "Gun!" she announced.

Vic and Webb hurried to look. Erin pointed. A black automatic pistol lay there, sleek and deadly.

"Beretta 92," Vic said. "Nine-millimeter." He had an encyclopedic knowledge of firearms.

"That's a match for the casing," Webb said. "Has it been fired recently?"

Erin had been trying not to breathe through her nose. She steeled herself and took a whiff, managing not to retch.

"Yeah," she said. "Smells like gunpowder."

"Okay," Webb said with a smile. He had a reason to look pleased. Finding the murder weapon was a huge break. "Looks like we got the murder weapon. Don't touch it, O'Reilly. But can you see anything on it?"

Erin examined the pistol. "No silencer," she said. "I'm surprised no one heard the shots. The magazine's still in it, so it's probably loaded. Serial number is intact."

"Really?" Vic asked, bending closer. Criminals often filed the number off a weapon to make it harder to track.

"Great," Webb said. "Get a picture and run the number, see who it's registered to."

"It'll be stolen," Vic predicted.

"It's still a place to start," Webb said.

*   *   *

If Doctor Levine had been woken up, or pulled away from some social event, it wasn't obvious from how she looked. She was wearing her usual lab coat, scrubs, and slightly distracted expression.

"Where's the dead guy?" she asked by way of greeting.

Vic indicated Caleb's body with a thumb. Levine walked straight to him, knelt down, and started her examination.

While Levine worked, Erin went back to the Charger and entered the serial number of the Beretta into her onboard computer. She was pretty sure it would be a waste of time. Like Vic had said, it would almost certainly be stolen. But it was good to cross all the T's.

The pistol was registered all right. For the second time that night, Erin felt the world fall out from under her feet.

"No," she said softly. But there it was, right on her screen.

The pistol was registered to Ian Thompson.

Erin got back out of her car and walked toward the other two detectives on feet that felt twice as heavy as usual. When she got there, Levine had just stood up and was talking to Webb.

"Preliminary cause of death is a single gunshot wound at close range," Levine said. "It appears to be a nine-millimeter handgun round, entrance wound just above the bridge of the nose. Death was instantaneous."

"I didn't see any powder marks," Webb observed. "Why do you say close range?"

"One wound?" Vic asked. "Doc, I know I haven't got a medical degree, but this guy's got two bullet holes in him."

"One shot, close range, like I said," Levine said with a hint of irritation. "Note the powder tattooing on the palm of the hand. Also note the blood spatter on the face."

"He held his hand in front of his face," Webb said, nodding.

"Tried to catch the bullet," Vic said. "That never ends well."

"The bullet transited the palm and entered the forehead," Levine said. "On the basis of the powder marks on the palm, the shot was fired within one meter of the victim."

"That's risky," Vic said. "The whole point of a gun is so you don't have to stand right next to a guy when you smoke him."

"And our victim's a big guy," Webb added. "A little on the pudgy side, but he still looks like he was pretty strong. Maybe our victim made a play for the gun, grabbed at it, and got shot. Anything else, Doctor?"

"The face, arms, and hands show significant discoloration," Levine said. "It's indicative of ante-mortem bruising."

"He was beaten before being shot," Webb said. "Can you tell what did the damage?"

"Blunt force impacts," Levine said. "Nothing cylindrical or with sharp corners. I'll want to check under better lighting, but it appears he was struck with fists. I see marks consistent with knuckle impacts, though the bruising is unusually severe for bare-hand strikes."

Erin made herself look closer at Caleb's face. Levine was right. One eye was puffy and swollen and the nose looked crooked.

"That's weird," Vic said. "If he got beat up before being shot, why weren't his hands tied?"

"Maybe he broke free and got shot trying to escape," Webb said doubtfully.

"The wrists show no ligature marks," Levine said. "I see no evidence the subject was restrained."

"Got anything on the gun, O'Reilly?" Webb asked.

"It's registered to Ian Thompson," she said quietly.

There were a few seconds of dead silence.

Vic whistled. "We had him in custody," he said. "This morning. He was in a holding cell less than twelve hours ago!"

"We couldn't hold him and you know it," Webb said. "Looks like Carlyle's people are turning on each other."

"We don't know it was Ian," Erin said.

"No, I guess not," Vic said, sarcasm dripping from every word. "It was probably some other guy, using Thompson's gun, to kill Thompson's coworker, in back of the restaurant owned by Thompson's boss. Yeah, that makes sense."

"This doesn't fit the way Ian operates," she argued, but it sounded weak even to her. "He doesn't just execute people. He's not on the muscle side of the O'Malleys. Hell, he's not even directly affiliated with them."

"He's doing a good job faking it," Vic said.

"Look," Webb said. "I know he helped you out, O'Reilly. And maybe you feel like you owe him one. I get that. You don't have to be there when we go get him. Neshenko will bring him in."

"Sir," Erin protested.

Webb held up his hand. "I misspoke. I don't *want* you there. You're emotionally compromised with respect to Thompson. Hell, you probably shouldn't be on this case at all."

"You can't bench me!"

"I can, and I will if you make it necessary," he said grimly. "If I think you're doing anything that jeopardizes this investigation, you're done. Are we clear?"

Erin glared at him, but being angry didn't shut down all her brain cells. "Copy that, sir," she said. He did have a point. And that wasn't the most important thing at the moment. She turned to Vic.

"Vic? Don't go in heavy. He's not going to fight you."

"He better not," Vic growled. "We got his address?"

"It's in his file from last night," Webb said. "With the weapon in his name, there won't be any problem getting a warrant."

"Let me go along," Erin insisted. "This is my job, sir, and my responsibility."

"You gonna be my babysitter?" Vic sneered. "I'm not the one who needs watching."

"You'll want backup, Neshenko," Webb said. "I'll supervise CSU here. Take two Patrol units... and O'Reilly and her K-9. But O'Reilly, you don't go into his apartment. Not unless shots are fired. You understand? You're observing only. Take Neshenko with you in your car."

Erin gritted her teeth. "Yes, sir."

Chapter 5

Ian Thompson lived on the third floor of a brick walk-up apartment just a few blocks from the Barley Corner. It was an old building, but clean and in good repair. Vic, in the passenger seat of Erin's Charger, strapped on his Kevlar vest.

"He's not going to resist," Erin said. She didn't want Vic to shoot Ian.

"Then we won't have a problem," Vic said. He got out of the car. Four uniformed officers had followed them in a pair of squad cars. They circled up around Vic for instructions. Erin got out of the Charger and leaned against it, holding Rolf and feeling frustrated and useless.

"Okay," Vic said. "This guy's a combat veteran. He's killed people, overseas and right here at home. We're going in hard and fast. As long as he cooperates, we're fine. But if he goes for a weapon, you put him on the ground. Don't hesitate, just do it. Copy?"

"Copy," said all four officers. One of them, the youngest, raised her hand.

"Yeah?" Vic prompted.

"Shouldn't this be a job for ESU?"

Vic snorted. "Nah, we got this. You, what's your name?"

"Plunkett, sir," said the officer he pointed to.

"You're going first. Knock, give him about three seconds. If he doesn't acknowledge, take the door. I'll be right behind you." Vic slapped a full magazine into his M4 rifle and chambered a round. "If we take fire, don't panic. Check your target, get clean shots, use cover. Okay, people. They don't pay us to sit on our asses. O'Reilly," he added, as if just now remembering she was there. "Why don't you hang streetside. Keep an eye on the fire escape and windows. He may want to play Peter Pan."

Erin seethed. She outranked Vic and was under no obligation to take his orders. "Copy that," she said. "Easy on that trigger finger, Vic."

"I don't start fights," he said. "I just finish 'em."

Erin and Rolf watched their fellow officers go into the building. Erin hoped Vic would exercise some restraint. He didn't like Ian, didn't trust him. But Vic wasn't a murderer. If Ian gave up and came quietly, he wouldn't get shot. Probably.

She looked up at the building and tried to guess which window belonged to Ian's apartment. Most of them were dark. After all, it was going on midnight. But apparently a few night owls were still awake. She'd know if there was shooting by the sounds and the muzzle flashes. She paced nervously from one end of her parked car to the other.

Rolf padded at her side, looking up at her. His tail waved uncertainly. He knew their job was to be up there with the other cops, kicking doors open, grabbing perps. He didn't understand what they were doing out here where nothing was going on.

Erin listened and waited. The team must be upstairs by now, stacking up in the hallway outside the apartment. She heard nothing, just the ordinary nighttime sounds of Manhattan on the street. Total silence was a rare thing in the big city.

She opened her car door and got her radio handset out, holding it at the end of its cord. She wanted to call, to ask what was happening, but she knew she'd just get chewed out by Vic for distracting him and maybe tipping off the guy they'd come to arrest.

The thought hit her, for the first time in her twelve-year career, that she could call Ian and warn him. She genuinely believed he had no intention of shooting it out with the NYPD, but if someone kicked in his door in the middle of the night, his combat instincts might take over. He could go for a gun, in which case the only possible outcome was that someone was going to get hurt. Worst-case scenario, he might kill a cop in misguided self-defense and get mowed down. Maybe Vic and Ian were both about to die. What a damned mess.

She didn't know Ian's phone number. Besides, what the hell was she thinking, calling a murder suspect ahead of a police raid? They'd find her call in his phone history. Then she'd be screwed, too.

"Damn it," she muttered. She hadn't even started on her undercover assignment, and already she could hardly tell what she was supposed to do.

Something was happening on the third floor. Erin saw the curtain on the third window from the right twitch slightly open. The room remained dark. That suggested it might be Ian; he'd know better than to wreck his night vision by turning on a light.

Erin raised a hand and waved, not knowing whether he was looking or not. If he recognized her, he'd know the police presence was genuine. Then maybe he wouldn't fight.

The curtain fell back into place. A few seconds later, the light came on. Erin saw it as a faint glow around the edge of the window, almost completely absorbed by the heavy drapes of a man who worked nights and slept by day. She imagined the officers flooding into the room, checking the corners, clearing the apartment, throwing Ian down on the floor and cuffing him. She clenched her fists helplessly. They could have just asked him to come in and he'd have come. This whole thing was risky and unnecessary.

The radio in her hand crackled to life. "Dispatch, this is Neshenko. Got one in custody. We need a CSU team to collect evidence."

"Copy that, Neshenko," Dispatch replied.

Erin let out a breath she hadn't known she'd been holding. She hadn't heard any shots. Everyone was still alive.

Vic came out with two of the Patrol officers a few minutes later. The other two had presumably stayed behind to secure the apartment. The cops had Ian between them, in handcuffs. They'd allowed him to put on shoes, but he was wearing only a white T-shirt and a pair of dark gray shorts. Most people, pulled out of bed by police at midnight, would be frightened and upset. Ian was stone-cold calm. He glanced at Erin but gave no sign of recognition.

"Everything go okay?" Erin asked Vic.

"Yeah," he said, sounding a little disappointed. "Guy answered the door when we knocked. Nothing in his hands, but it was like he was waiting for us. Guess he figured he'd done enough for one night." He pointed to one of the uniforms. "You want to take this happy asshole back to the Eightball? We got a dog in our back seat."

"Sure thing," the cop said.

"Any sign of anything in the apartment?" Erin asked.

"He's got a gun rack in his bedroom," Vic said. "Guy's armed to the friggin' teeth. I swear his permits aren't legit."

"I've checked him before," Erin said. "He's licensed, and I'll bet any gun he's got at his place is legally his."

"He's not so smart," Vic said. "Not if he's popping guys with his personal handguns. Drive."

"I'm not your chauffeur."

"Maybe not. But you're the one with the car keys, and we're just sitting here. You planning to hang out on the street all night?"

Erin started the Charger. "Vic, I'm on your side," she said. "Stop trying to pick a fight."

He grunted a sound that might have meant anything.

"Did you see his hands?" Erin asked.

"Yeah."

"Any marks on the knuckles?"

"Not that I saw. But maybe he had on gloves. Or maybe he had an accomplice. Hell, maybe this Carnahan punk got in another fight earlier and the marks on his face didn't have anything to do with him getting shot."

"Are you planning on explaining away everything that doesn't fit your theory on what you want to have happened?"

"You trying to pick a fight now, O'Reilly?" he retorted. "I'm planning on clearing this case and locking up a bad guy."

"He saved my life," Erin said softly. "Maybe more than once."

"You think that makes him a hero? Jesus, for all we know, Mob guys help little old ladies cross the street and pull kittens out of trees. You think that gives them a pass to do whatever the hell they want? Erin, a guy can be a good citizen every damn day of his life but one, and when he crosses that line we still gotta drag his ass downtown."

"I know. It just doesn't feel right. I don't like him for this, Vic. Something else is going on here."

"You're getting blinded by your feelings."

"And you're not?"

"What's that supposed to mean?"

Erin shook her head. "Forget about it. Let's just get this over with."

* * *

"Do you know why you're here, punk?"

Vic was in Ian's face in the interrogation room. He and Webb were conducting things, while Erin and Rolf watched from the observation room. If they were running the traditional good cop/bad cop routine, Erin was willing to bet Vic wasn't playing good cop.

Ian didn't shy away from the big Russian, but he didn't return the other man's scowl, either. "You showed me the warrant," he said calmly.

"Murder, tough guy," Vic said. "You just can't help it, can you? Why'd you do it this time? You got another bullshit excuse about protecting someone?"

"I gave you my report last night," Ian said. "Nothing's changed since then."

"I'm not talking about last night, dumbass!" Vic shouted. "I'm talking about the guy you popped a couple hours ago! The morgue downstairs is getting pretty goddamned full, all because of you!"

"What's he talking about, sir?" Ian asked, turning to Webb with an expression of polite interest.

"Look, Mr. Thompson," Webb said. "I understand you've been through a rough time overseas, and I thank you for your service to this country. We've both worn uniforms and carried guns to protect America. We're not as different as all that. The Marines trained you well. You're good at what you do. And I understand you believe in doing what's right. I just need to know why you did what you did. We didn't charge you when you shot that Colombian earlier this year, and we released you this morning after the shootout at Erin's apartment. You had good reasons for both those shootings. Tell me why you killed this guy and we can sort all this out."

"What guy are you talking about, sir?"

"You kill more than one tonight?" Vic asked.

"I've killed quite a few people, sir," Ian said, still talking to Webb. "But no one today."

"You were picked up at this station by a car with two guys in it," Webb said. "Caleb Carnahan and Michael Connor. Where did they take you?"

"I'd prefer not to answer that question, sir."

"Your preferences don't mean shit!" Vic snarled. "You're looking at Murder One. If you can't give us a rock solid, airtight alibi, you're lunch meat, pal!"

"What time period are we talking about, sir?" Ian asked Webb.

"We're talking about today," Webb said. "The whole day. When did you leave Carnahan and Connor's company?"

"I didn't kill anyone today, sir."

"That's not what I asked. Where were you?" Webb's voice became softer, more coaxing. "Don't you understand? I want to help you, but if you won't help me, I can't help you."

"No assistance needed, sir."

Webb sighed. "Do you own a Beretta 92 semiautomatic pistol, black in color?"

"Yes, sir. Two of them, both legally registered in my name with permits for concealed carry."

"Where are those guns right now?"

"You have one of them in your evidence locker, sir, unless I'm mistaken. Your officers confiscated it from me last night. I can't locate the other one."

"You lost your gun?"

"I didn't lose it, sir. I can't locate it."

Vic snorted audibly.

"Where did you last see it?" Webb asked.

"In my locker in my apartment, sir."

"Did you check your locker today, after you got home?"

"Yes, sir."

"Was this gun in it?"

"No, sir."

"You expect us to believe that?" Vic interjected. "We checked your locker, too. It's full of guns and a shitload of ammo. You telling us someone broke in and just swiped the one gun?"

Ian shrugged. "No explanation. The Beretta wasn't there today."

"Does anyone else have keys to your gun locker?" Webb asked.

"No, sir."

"What about apartment keys?"

"The landlord, sir. No one else."

"You got any family?"

Ian shrugged again.

"Answer the question, dipshit," Vic growled.

"I'm not in touch with any family, sir," Ian said to Webb.

"Your dad's listed as next of kin," Webb said. He had Ian's military service file on the table in front of him.

"They needed to list someone, sir. They wouldn't take a non-relative."

"So you're not on good terms with your dad?" Webb asked.

"Haven't spoken to him in a few years, sir."

"How many?"

Another shrug. "Eight, give or take. Not since I joined the Corps."

"Do you like Mickey Connor?" Webb asked, changing subjects abruptly. Erin knew this was a deliberate technique, designed to keep suspects off balance.

"Don't know him well, sir."

"What about Caleb Carnahan?"

"No opinion, sir."

"You've worked for Carlyle a few years now," Webb said. "Caleb's in charge of security for your boss. You handle Carlyle's personal protection. You have to have an opinion of him."

"The Corps taught me not to have opinions of superior officers, sir," Ian said placidly. "It's bad for morale."

"How about fragging officers?" Vic asked. "The Corps teach you to do that, too?"

"Only officers I ever took out were tangos," Ian said, using the military slang for enemy combatants.

"Got any tangos here in the States?" Vic asked.

"I'm not in the Corps anymore. I'm on a security detail, not search and destroy."

"Do you think Caleb's been doing a good job, protecting your boss?" Webb asked.

"Mr. Carlyle's still alive," Ian said, as if that was answer enough.

"He's alive only because you and Erin O'Reilly took out an assassin, and because he got some top-notch medical attention," Webb said. "Caleb wasn't there. He didn't warn you of any trouble. It was his fault this whole thing happened, wasn't it?"

"No opinion, sir."

"If something happens to Caleb, who takes over Carlyle's security?" Webb asked, with another shift.

"Not my call, sir. You'd have to ask Mr. Carlyle."

"You want the job?" Vic challenged.

"I like my job," Ian replied.

"Look, numbnuts, you got a smart answer for everything," Vic said. "How about this? We got a dead body in an alley, killed with your gun, with your fingerprints on it. We know you shot Carnahan, so stop wasting our goddamn time!"

Ian blinked once. "Mr. Carnahan's dead, sir?" he asked Webb.

Webb and Vic both stared at him. So did Erin. She was trying to read that flat, serious poker face. Was he surprised to hear of Caleb's death? Had he killed Caleb? She knew Ian better than the other detectives did, and even she wasn't sure.

Her phone buzzed in her hip pocket. Cursing to herself at the interruption, she pulled it out and saw an unknown number. Could it be Carlyle, on a new phone? Or something else?

"O'Reilly," she said, answering but keeping her eyes on the interrogation room.

"I'm glad I could reach you," said a distinctly Irish voice, but it wasn't Carlyle's. It was colder, harder. She'd heard that voice before. It was Evan O'Malley, Carlyle's boss.

"How'd you get this number, Mr. O'Malley?" she asked.

"Through a mutual acquaintance," Evan said. "I'm thinking we need to have a conversation, Miss O'Reilly. At your earliest possible convenience."

Erin's mind and heartrate both went into overdrive. "I'm working right now," she said.

"As am I," he said. "If you can make time in your busy schedule, I'll be grateful."

"It's pretty late," she said, stalling for time. "Maybe first thing in the morning?"

"I'm awake," he said. "And will be, for the foreseeable future. When might you become available?"

Erin saw Vic and Webb still hammering away at Ian. He was giving them nothing useful.

"I don't know," she said. "Maybe another couple of hours?"

"I'll have a car waiting for you down the street," Evan said. "Black Lincoln. They'll be expecting you."

He hung up without waiting for her confirmation. Erin stared at the phone. This was it. Time to take a deep breath and dive. There were only three subjects. Evan might conceivably want to talk to her about: Siobhan Finneran, Caleb Carnahan, or

Morton Carlyle. She needed to think, and think fast. Her life and Carlyle's might both depend on what she said and did in the next few hours.

In the interrogation room, things weren't going well. Vic was practically foaming at the mouth, trying to provoke a reaction. Webb was patient and reassuring. Ian kept politely answering Webb's questions, being neither helpful nor confrontational, and ignoring Vic whenever possible.

"This is getting us nowhere," Webb said.

"I agree, sir," Ian said. "Am I dismissed?"

"You're about to be charged with first-degree murder," Webb said. "You're not going anywhere."

"In that case, sir, with all due respect, I'd like to exercise my right to an attorney."

And that was it. Erin had a few moments to herself, while the other detectives got their papers together. She pulled out the phone Phil Stachowski had given her and called the contact labeled Leo.

"Can you talk freely?" Phil asked, picking up on the third ring. He sounded a little sleepy, but more or less alert.

"Yeah, but it needs to be quick," Erin said. "Listen, I just got a call from Evan O'Malley. He wants to meet."

"When?" Phil sounded completely awake now. Erin heard a door open in the background, then close.

"Now. As soon as I can. He's got guys outside the Eightball waiting for me."

"Do you know where they're taking you?"

"No."

"Okay. Stay calm, Erin. If the boss himself called, he's not intending to hurt you. He wouldn't have risked putting his voice over the phone if he was. So this is just a conversation. Remember to come across as genuine, but you don't have to agree to everything he asks. You're playing the part of a dirty cop, so think like one. Be selfish. Be greedy. Be what he expects you to be and you'll be fine. You've got this, Erin."

She swallowed. "Okay."

"And call me once you're safe, Erin. Just make sure no one's listening when you do."

"Copy that. Thanks."

"Don't mention it, Erin. It's what I'm here for. Good luck."

Chapter 6

"I'm not sure he's our guy," Erin said.

"It's his gun," Vic said. "He knew Carnahan. Hell, they worked together. Carnahan screwed up, Carlyle almost got whacked, Thompson got pissed. He had motive, he sure as hell had means, and you know yourself he had opportunity. You saw him get in a car with the guy, for God's sake! He's one of the last people to see him alive. What more do you want?"

"It's pretty compelling," Webb agreed. "Definitely enough to charge him. CSU is going over Thompson's apartment. Maybe they'll find more."

"I didn't see any sign of forced entry," Vic added. "His gun locker was closed and locked."

"There's skeleton keys and lockpicks," Erin argued.

"He had powder residue on him," Vic said.

"I know he fired a gun less than two days ago!" she shot back. "I saw him do it!"

"You're just defending him because he protected you!"

Erin glared at him. It was more than that. This wasn't Ian's style. But then, how well did she know him, really? When he'd been a Marine, he would have killed enemies however he could.

And what if he'd taken Caleb out because she'd told him to? Was she refusing to accept the evidence because Ian's guilt would make her guilty, too? She'd be an accessory to murder, morally and maybe even legally.

"Good work tonight, everyone," Webb said. "It's late, we all need to get some rest. Go home and sleep. We'll take another look at it in the morning, but this case will keep until then. Neshenko, good job on the takedown. O'Reilly, excellent work locating the weapon."

Erin and Vic muttered acknowledgment of Webb's praise. They left the Major Crimes office without speaking to one another. Even if they'd been in a good place, Erin might not have wanted to share what was on her mind.

She didn't go to the garage. Instead, she went out the front door of Precinct 8. She paused a moment on the stairs and looked up and down the block. Sure enough, a dark-colored Town Car sat at the curb at a discreet distance.

"Ready for this, kiddo?" she asked Rolf.

Rolf wagged his tail. He was always ready.

Erin squared her shoulders and started down the block toward the waiting car. She tried to think how a dirty cop would handle the approach. Should she swagger up, all confidence and bravado? Should she act shifty? Scared? Angry? A lot was riding on this meeting.

"You're overthinking, O'Reilly," she muttered under her breath. She'd already met the O'Malley leadership. She was a cop, not an actress. She needed to be herself, just with a twist. She had to seem willing to compromise her principles for the sake of her relationship with Carlyle. And maybe, with what was happening, that was truer than she wanted it to be. Maybe she wasn't playing a part at all.

As she approached the Town Car, the rear passenger door swung open. An enormous man rose out of the car like a bad dream.

"Evening, Mickey," Erin said in as level a voice as she could manage.

Mickey Connor's lip twisted in an expression that couldn't possibly be mistaken for a smile. "Get in," he said.

"I will, as soon as you shift your ass out of my way," Erin said. She knew the underworld ran on reputation, image, and perception. She couldn't afford for Mickey to think she was afraid of him. She was, of course. Her fight-or-flight response engaged, like it did every time she saw that guy at close quarters. He was the most physically intimidating man she'd ever met, six feet six inches of muscle and brutality. Word on the street was that he didn't like to carry a gun. It wasn't like he needed one. He was a retired heavyweight boxer. The only weapons he habitually had on him were two rolls of quarters, one in each pocket, to load his fists with extra power. Erin figured she could take him from a distance, but up close, even with a gun in her hand, she didn't like her odds.

Evan only wanted to talk, she reminded herself. She put a hand on her hip and waited, staring at Mickey. He held her look with his flat, pale eyes. Finally, he shifted his bulk to make room for her to slide into the back seat of the car. Erin climbed in. Her K-9 waited on the sidewalk, eyeing Mickey suspiciously.

"Rolf! *Hupf!*" she ordered, pointing to the car seat. Rolf obediently jumped up beside her, making a buffer between her and Mickey, who squeezed in and closed the door. The driver started the car and pulled away from the curb. Rolf bristled at Mickey's close proximity.

"Where are we going?" Erin asked.

Mickey didn't answer.

It was just another power play, she knew that. If it was supposed to make her feel vulnerable, it didn't work. She just felt irritated. "There's no bag over my head," she said. "I'm going to see where it is anyway."

"You wearin' a wire?" Mickey asked.

Erin knew how to answer that one. "Screw you!" she snapped. "No, I'm not wearing a goddamn wire. I bet you'd just love to pat me down, but you try that, you're losing fingers."

"You got a smart mouth on you," he said. "A little smarter and you'd know when to keep it shut."

"Or somebody shuts it for me?"

"Or I find something to put in it."

"Anything you stick in my mouth, you're not getting back," she told him. Erin wasn't quite as confident as she sounded, but she thought she'd probably be okay. He might hate her, but as long as Evan found her useful, Mickey had no choice but to leave her alone.

The Town Car pulled up to an office building. Erin made a mental note of the address. Mickey got out and gestured with a sideways tilt of his head for her to follow him. She and Rolf obeyed.

Mickey was walking ahead of her, which was good. Mob assassins preferred to strike from behind. Erin didn't see any other goons until they entered the lobby. Then she saw a pair of guys loitering by the elevators. They looked like burly construction workers. Both men sported tattoos that looked like jailhouse ink.

"Fifteenth floor," Mickey said, pointing to the nearest elevator. Erin, Rolf, and he got in. She punched the number 15 and the car started to climb.

"No guns," he said suddenly.

"Forget about it," Erin said. "Your boss called me. I'm not going to whip out my Glock and blow him away. Cool your jets."

"That's the rules," Mickey said. He shifted his weight slightly, and he was suddenly more menacing. Erin could see from the way he stood that he was lighter on his feet than any guy his size ought to be. His balance was superb. She needed to remember he wasn't just a big thug. He'd been a professional athlete.

"Your rules, not mine," she said, not giving an inch. She was trying to build her persona for the O'Malleys. She needed to show them she wasn't a pushover, or they'd never respect her. Worse, they'd expect her to do all sorts of crap for them, probably illegal. If she rolled over for them, she was done.

"Give," he said. "Or I'm gonna take what I want."

"You lay a finger on me and Rolf's going to tear your nuts off," she promised. "Then I'll shove my piece in the hole where they used to be and empty the clip."

Mickey smiled. It was a terrifying expression that didn't go anywhere near his eyes. "Now that I'd like to see," he said. But he didn't touch her.

The elevator hit the fifteenth floor and stopped. Mickey led the way through what looked like a typical white-collar office to a conference room. Another no-neck goon was standing at the door. He nodded to Mickey and opened it.

Whenever Erin entered the Barley Corner, Carlyle would always stand to greet her. He was an old-school gentleman who never forgot his manners. Evan O'Malley, on the other hand, remained seated and watched Erin from the far end of a dark wood conference table. His hands were clasped on the tabletop, his Notre Dame school ring glinting on the fourth finger of his right hand. Evan was a hard-faced, cold-eyed Irishman who could have passed for the CEO of a thoroughly nasty corporation. Which, come to think of it, was pretty much what he was.

"Thank you, Mr. Connor," Evan said. "That will be all for now. Please close the door on your way."

Mickey didn't look happy to be leaving Erin alone with his boss, but he wasn't dumb enough to protest. He gave her one last look and stepped outside. The door swung shut behind him.

"Thank you for coming on such short notice, Miss O'Reilly," Evan said. "I understand it's late, and you're surely tired. Please, sit down."

"I'm fine," Erin said. She considered remaining standing, but decided it would be rude, and rudeness to this man might be suicidal. She sat. Rolf kept his eyes trained on his partner. Since she was sitting quietly, he did the same, awaiting orders.

"I assume you've looked in on Cars," he went on. "How is he?"

Erin studied Evan's face, trying to read whether he'd been the one to order the attack. "He'll make it," she said.

"That's grand news," Evan said. "Is there anything he might be needing?"

"We're good," she said and almost instantly second-guessed herself. Should she act greedier? But it was already too late. The words were out and she couldn't backpedal.

"I've received a fairly comprehensive report of what happened in your flat," he said. "Have you anything to add?"

Erin decided how to play it. The best lies, she knew, were ninety percent truth. "I want to know which of your guys tried to have my boyfriend whacked," she said, meeting his cold-eyed stare and letting him see the anger in her. It wasn't difficult to show.

"Miss O'Reilly, I assure you, I'd nothing to do with the unpleasantness," he said. "If any of my people have exceeded their authority, I'll see the situation is taken care of. You needn't trouble yourself."

That was eerily similar to what Ian had said about Caleb. "Thanks," she said. "I assume you didn't bring me here just to ask after Carlyle's health?"

"We need to clarify a few matters," Evan said. "You've been operating on the fringes of my interests for some time, Miss O'Reilly, with a certain amount of personal success. You've been something of a mixed blessing to me and mine. On the one hand, you've dealt with some rather unpleasant individuals who might have caused me a great deal of trouble. On the other, I've noticed that those lads who come in contact with you are putting themselves in particular peril of being shot or incarcerated."

"If you're talking about Tommy Jay," Erin said, referring to Evan's nephew, currently doing time upstate, "he hired guys behind your back with the intention of destabilizing the underworld and taking over your business. I did you a favor by locking him up."

"Whereas Liam McIntyre, Siobhan Finneran, and a number of others were prematurely retired from their positions," he said dryly.

"I didn't kill Liam," she objected. "He brought that on himself, double-dealing with those Colombians. But I did take care of the guys who did it. And Siobhan tried to kill me. You think I asked her to break into my place and try to shoot me? Hell, she *did* shoot Carlyle."

One corner of Evan's mouth moved slightly. It might have been a hint of a smile, or maybe just an involuntary muscle twitch. "Nonetheless, you can't deny there's a pattern."

"It's a dangerous world," she said with a deliberately callous shrug. She knew Evan was a stone-cold psychopath. Showing human weakness would only earn his contempt.

Evan nodded thoughtfully. "It seems you've formed quite an attachment to my lad," he said. "We're both glad he's doing well. It's true, you've been of some service to my interests. But I've also been told you're not entirely trustworthy. Can you tell me, Miss O'Reilly, why I should trust you?"

"Trust me? You shouldn't," she said, remembering what Carlyle had told her about Evan. He'd said Evan was a man who didn't trust anyone. "You don't know me, and I don't know you. But if you won't take Carlyle's word when he vouches for me, I don't think there's anything I can say that'll make you think different."

It was a risky thing to say, but Erin was confident it was the right one. To get in with the Mob, she needed someone already on the inside to speak for her. That carried far more weight than anything else she could bring.

"I understand your people have arrested Ian Thompson," he said. "Again."

"Yeah."

"You'll take care of it?"

Erin blinked and tried to figure out what, exactly, Evan was asking her to do. "I'm working on it," she said, hedging. "I got him out this morning."

"And he was back inside by bedtime."

She considered what to say. Evan wasn't really asking about Ian. He didn't care what happened to Ian, as long as the bodyguard kept his mouth shut. What he was really asking was how much power Erin had to influence events at her precinct, and how much of that power she was prepared to put to work on the O'Malleys' behalf.

She decided to answer the same way he'd asked, indirectly. She silently thanked Carlyle for teaching her this style of conversation. She'd demonstrate that she had inside information she was willing to release. That would speak to her value.

"My people think Ian shot Caleb Carnahan a couple hours ago," she said, breaking the NYPD's rules about releasing information about ongoing investigations.

"And why, exactly, would they think that?" Evan asked.

"We found his gun at the scene."

"Ah," Evan said, steepling his fingers. "That is awkward. But evidence, even hard evidence, is something of a slippery thing."

"The gun's already locked up at the Eightball," she said. "And the serial number is on file. But Ian's a stand-up guy. And he's one of Carlyle's best people. I'm going to help him. But there's something you can do for me, too."

"And what might that be?"

"You can make sure your shooters don't come after me anymore."

Evan's eyes got even colder. "I'll attend to my business, Miss O'Reilly. You attend to yours. I'm sure I don't need to explain this to you, but our business, as all others, is founded on reciprocity. It's my understanding that you are in a position of some influence. Should your department become embroiled in the workings of my organization, I'll be forced to draw certain conclusions regarding your intentions."

"I understand completely, Mr. O'Malley," she said, hoping that was true.

"Excellent." Now he did stand up, indicating the interview was over. Erin did likewise. So did Rolf, taking his cue from her. "I'm glad to speak to you face to face," he went on. "There's just one other small matter to attend to. I understand Mr. Carlyle is at Bellevue Hospital?"

"That's right." There was no point denying it.

"I should like to make a delivery to his room. You know the sort of thing. Flowers, a sentimental card. But I believe he's under police protection. Could you, perhaps, facilitate this delivery?"

"I'd be happy to, sir," Erin said. Then, as a thought struck her, "Why don't you have Corky Corcoran drop them off? I know his face, so I'll know for sure he's coming from you. I can get him past the guard."

"Excellent," Evan said. He walked around the table toward her and extended his hand. Erin shook it. His skin was dry, his grip firm. His fingernails were filed smooth. It was an executive's hand. Erin wondered how many people he'd killed with it.

"You have a good night, Mr. O'Malley," Erin said.

"And you, Miss O'Reilly. Oh, just one more thing. It nearly slipped my mind."

Not a chance, Erin thought. Nothing slipped Evan's mind. "What's that?" she asked.

"I'll be hosting a small gathering at my city apartment, the day after tomorrow, at nine o' clock in the evening. Nothing particularly grand or formal, just a social get-together. We'll play a few hands of cards for the usual stakes. I'd appreciate it if you'd attend."

"Carlyle's still going to be in the hospital," she said.

"I'm inviting you." His mouth smiled. His eyes remained unchanged.

"I'll need the address."

"I'm sure you'll find it." He looked down at Rolf. "Magnificent animal, exceptionally trained. Personally, I find the balance between discipline and savagery fascinating. Mr. Connor will be glad to take you wherever you wish to go. Good evening, Miss O'Reilly."

* * *

"Guess the boss likes you," Mickey commented on the elevator ride down.

"What makes you say that?" Erin asked. She didn't want to get in a conversation with him, didn't even want to be within twenty feet of him, but she had to be alert to every opportunity to gain information about the O'Malleys.

He shrugged his massive shoulders. "We're goin' back out the front way."

She felt a chill. She had the feeling she could guess what might have happened if Evan didn't like her. She reminded herself what Phil had told her. Evan was smart. He wouldn't have put himself on the line to have her whacked. He had people for that. People like the goon riding the elevator with her.

"I guess you've handled it both ways," she said.

"I do what's gotta be done."

The elevator reached the ground floor. The doors slid open and they walked to the waiting car. Erin opened the door herself, not bothering to wait and see whether Mickey would do the polite thing or not.

"Back to the station?" he asked.

"Yeah."

"You got that?" Mickey asked the driver.

"Sure thing, chief," the man said.

"Rolf, *hupf!*" Erin ordered. The Shepherd hopped into the back seat with her. She reached past him for the door handle.

Mickey's hand, the size of a canned ham, closed on the doorframe, holding the door open. He bent down so their eyes met.

"Careful, O'Reilly. The boss likes you now, but maybe in a week or a month he won't. I'll be watching. And waiting."

He let go of the door.

Chapter 7

Mickey's driver dropped Erin and Rolf half a block from Precinct 8 and drove away. Erin made a mental note of the Town Car's license plate. She had no intention of running the plates, but Patrol habits were hard to break. She watched the car disappear into the late-night Manhattan traffic. Then she went down to the parking garage to get her Charger.

She loaded Rolf into his compartment in back. Then she slipped behind the wheel, closed the door, and pulled out the phone Phil had given her. She opened the contact list.

What if her car was bugged?

That was a crazy thought. It was an official NYPD vehicle. There was no way anyone had put a surveillance device on it. The precinct's garage was secure.

What if it wasn't? The O'Malleys could have more than one source in the NYPD. Besides, Erin's apartment garage wasn't nearly as secure as the one at the Eightball. And, of course, a Mob assassin had recently been in her home.

That was crazy, Erin repeated to herself. If there was a listening device, it would have been planted by Internal Affairs, not by the Irish mob. And Lieutenant Keane already knew about her. He was on her side.

Wasn't he? She remembered what Phil had said about Keane. But she didn't completely trust Phil, either.

"Jesus," she muttered, letting her head sink down to rest her forehead against the steering wheel. Paranoia was a hole that just kept on going, deeper and darker. Give in to it once and it could drive a person nuts.

She decided being prudent wasn't the same thing as being paranoid and put the phone back in her pocket. She started the car and drove back to brother's house. After she parked, she released Rolf and took him across the street to the small neighborhood park. Once she'd made sure no one was lurking nearby, she got the phone out again and called Phil.

He answered before she'd even had time to wonder whether he'd gone to sleep.

"Everything all right?" he asked, sounding wide awake. He'd probably been waiting by the phone.

"Yeah." She thought for a second. "You know, maybe we should have a safeword in case things aren't okay. Maybe there's a guy standing behind me with a gun or something."

"That's a good thought, Erin. You're a natural at this."

"It's something Carlyle came up with," she said. "It saved my life this week."

"What word would you like to use?" he asked.

"How about Leo? That's the name in my contact list. If I ever call you that name, you'll know I've been made."

"Good plan. So, how did it go?"

"Fine. You were right, he just wanted to talk. He wants me to give some cover to the O'Malleys' operations. If I got his message right, he wants me to make sure Major Crimes doesn't infringe on his little empire."

"He wants you to compromise investigations to benefit his racket? He said that?"

"Not in so many words. He's cagey. But that's what he meant."

"Did he offer you anything in return?"

"No. I told him to keep his goons the hell away from me. That was the deal, for the moment. Oh, and I got invited to a card game."

"Social or business?"

"Both, I think. According to Carlyle, Evan and his guys get together about once a month to play cards. It's a cash game, but not much money by their standards. I think he does it to keep an eye on his guys and make sure he knows how they're doing. I've been to one before, at the Barley Corner."

"How was it?"

"A little nerve-wracking. Two of the guys almost got in a knife fight. You know how it is."

Phil laughed quietly. "You're something else, Erin. Where and when is the game going to be?"

"Nine in the evening, day after tomorrow. At Evan's place here in Manhattan."

"Really? Congratulations. Sounds like you're in."

"Maybe. I think he wants to see how I handle myself when Carlyle isn't around."

"Who else will be there?"

"O'Malley middle management." Erin thought back to her previous experience. "I expect Evan himself, Mickey Connor, James Corcoran, and Maggie Callahan. Maybe Veronica Blackburn. There were two others last time, Liam McIntyre and Carlyle, but Carlyle's in the hospital and Liam's dead. If Evan's got someone to take Liam's place, I guess I'll meet that guy."

"This is good, Erin. You've got your foot in the door. Just keep doing what you're doing. You know the main rules of undercover work."

She rolled her eyes. "Yeah. Don't kill anybody, don't promise anything I can't deliver, and don't do anything stupid."

"That about covers it. Thanks for calling back, Erin. If there's anything you need, let me know. I've got your back."

"Good to hear. I think maybe you're the only guy in the NYPD who does."

There was a pause long enough for Erin to regret saying that. She was tired, both from the late hour and the accumulated stress of the last couple of days, and it had just slipped out.

"You know who you are," Phil said. "That's going to need to be good enough to keep you going. Do you go to church?"

"Huh? Why?"

"If you've got belief in something higher than yourself, it can help keep you moving the right direction. Just like Alcoholics Anonymous. It's not necessary, but some of the people I've run through this kind of operation have said it helps."

"When all else fails, pray?" she asked, half-jokingly.

"It can't hurt," he replied.

"Are you religious?" she asked him.

"Roman Catholic. My dad's people came over from Poland about a hundred years back."

"I'm Catholic, too. Sort of."

"If that's a part of your life, draw on it. That's all I'm suggesting."

"I'll keep that in mind. Catch you later, Phil."

"Good night, Erin."

Erin quietly used the spare key to get into Sean and Michelle's home, tiptoeing up the stairs. It was almost two o' clock when she finally tumbled onto the air mattress they'd set out for her.

Rolf started circling, preparing to lie down near the foot of the mattress. Erin wasn't having any of that, not now. *"Komm,"* she whispered, patting the mattress next to her. Most K-9 handlers didn't hold with letting their partners in bed with them, preferring the discipline and distance of a dog crate at night. But Erin was with the minority on this one. And tonight she needed the reassurance of his warm, furry presence.

With one arm around her dog, she tried to put her worries away for a few hours. Remembering Phil's advice about faith, she said a quick prayer. Tomorrow would come soon enough, with plenty of problems. For now, Erin O'Reilly just prayed for uninterrupted sleep.

* * *

Erin woke from a nasty dream in which she'd been walking through Precinct 8. Every police officer saw silently turned and stared at her. They didn't say anything, but she knew that they *knew*. As she passed by, they began following her, first one at a time, then in a growing crowd. She walked faster, then started to run. As she ran down the concrete corridors, the hallways became narrower and narrower until she was squeezing frantically sideways.

She woke up short of breath. Rolf was lying with his head on her chest and she could hardly breathe. She heaved the big Shepherd off and got up. The K-9 followed her downstairs.

Her dad was in the kitchen, sipping a cup of coffee and reading the sports section of the Times. Without being asked, he got up and poured her a cup.

"Your mother knows something's up," he said quietly.

Erin sighed. "What'd you tell her?"

"I told her you were under a lot of stress and not to badger you. I told her you'd tell her what was on your mind when you were good and ready." He shook his head. "I don't like family secrets, kiddo."

"Sorry," she said. "Look, I can't hang around long. I need to swing by the hospital before work. I feel bad, with you two coming all the way down to the city and hardly seeing me."

"Forget about it," Sean said. "Your mother and I are having a nice visit with Junior, Shelley, and the grandkids. We'll be fine. You take care of yourself. And be careful."

Erin couldn't entirely suppress a snort. "Another guy told me that just a few hours ago."

"Cop?"

"No, a gangster. I'm pretty sure he was threatening to kill me."

Sean's eyes narrowed. "Are you in over your head, kiddo?"

"Up to my neck, Dad. But I'm still swimming. Love you." She gave him a hug and a kiss on the cheek. Then she was out the door. She knew Evan wouldn't be wasting time, so neither could she. She had to get to Bellevue ahead of his delivery. There were some things she needed to get clear with Carlyle.

* * *

Erin had no trouble with the guard at Carlyle's room, even with Rolf in tow. The man definitely considered his job a waste of time. He checked her ID in a perfunctory way and opened the door.

"They tell you why you're guarding this guy?" she asked him.

He shrugged. "The mope's under a John Doe. I'm guessing he's a witness, probably some gang member the DA hopes can ID the guy who popped him."

"Major Crimes wants him to stay alive," she said. As she went in, she made a point of looking at his shield to get his name and number. Hopefully that would help him take a little more interest in his work. "There may be a guy called Corcoran coming," she added. "Let him in. But he's the only one. Nobody else."

"Copy that," he said.

Erin went inside and closed the door as gently as she could. She told Rolf to watch the door. He settled on his haunches and did as she asked. Then she walked to Carlyle's bedside and looked down at him.

His eyes were closed and he appeared to be sleeping, but his face lacked the serenity it usually had when he was asleep. She saw lines of worry and pain drawn as deep as if they'd been carved with a knife. She reached for his hand and hesitated, not wanting to disturb him.

"I heard you come in, darling," he said softly.

"I'm sorry. I didn't mean to wake you."

"I'm having a bit of trouble staying asleep," he said, opening his eyes and smiling wryly. "A bullet in the belly will do that to a lad. What's happening?"

"Caleb Carnahan's dead," she said.

Carlyle's eyes opened a little wider, but he gave no other sign of surprise. "When? How?"

"Last night. Someone beat him up and shot him in the face. We found him behind the Barley Corner."

He nodded slowly. "That tells us one of two things. Either he was the traitor, or someone thinks he was."

"Or both," Erin agreed. "But it's possible this was just another attack on you and yours."

"There's little reason to be going after my security chief when I'm not there to be protected. Though God knows the lad had enemies."

"It's worse than that," she said, not wanting to say, but seeing no way around it.

"Then you'd best tell me and get it out in the open."

"How are you feeling?" she asked, stalling a little. "If you're in too much pain—"

"I'll be fine if you'll tell me what's bothering you. You're the one looking like you've a bullet in your guts right now." He took her hand with a surprisingly strong grip.

"We found the murder weapon in the trash next to the body," she said. "It's one of Ian's pistols."

Carlyle's face froze. Erin could see, whatever he'd been expecting, it hadn't been that. "Oh, no," he said softly.

"He's at the station," she went on. "Under arrest. And..." She almost choked on the next words. "I think maybe he did it. And if he did, I put him up to it."

"What? Darling, that's mad. You'd never have done anything of the sort!"

"But I did," she said miserably. "I told him not to trust Caleb and he said... he said he'd take care of it. I didn't mean... he had to know I didn't mean that!"

"Of course he knew," Carlyle said soothingly. "Listen, darling. I've known Ian since he was a wee lad of twelve, and I've never yet found a way to get him to do something he's not of a mind to do. Whatever he may have done, it wasn't because you told him to."

"But he got conditioned to obey orders by the Marines. Anyway, you don't think he killed Caleb, do you?"

Carlyle was silent.

"Oh, God," Erin muttered. "You do."

"The lad's capable of astonishing violence, Erin," he said gently. "He's killed men before, dozens of them. And he's minded to be protective of those he cares for. If he thought Caleb betrayed me, he'd have considered dispatching him at the very least. This is off the record, you understand, and I'll deny it if I have to, even under oath."

"I know," she said. Carlyle would sooner cut his own throat than testify against Ian. "But I think he may not have done it."

"Why not?"

"Ian's smart. He might have blown Caleb away, but he wouldn't have just left his gun, a gun that's registered in his name, right there at the scene. No way."

"That's hardly likely to convince a jury," he said. "But you make a good point as far as I'm concerned."

"It's all I've got. All the evidence points to him. I don't know whether there's something wrong with the evidence, or if I just don't want him to be the guy. I like him."

"As do I, darling. And you're right, it does seem a trifle unlikely. All you can do is your duty. Follow the evidence, find the truth. It's what you do. If your intuition is right, that's the best way you can save the lad. If it's not, then at least you'll know, and he'll be none the worse than he is now."

Erin, looking at Carlyle, was reminded that Mob guys took things like getting thrown in prison in their stride. It was a rare gangster who hadn't done a few years behind bars.

"There's something else," she said.

"You've had rather a busy night," he said.

"I talked to Evan last night. He's sending flowers."

"Is that all he's sending, I wonder?"

"I suggested he send Corky with them."

"Grand idea," he said. "If some other lad turns up with a bouquet, you'll know he's here to finish me off."

"Maybe I should leave you a piece, just in case. I don't think the guy out in the hall is exactly a shining example of New York's finest."

"I've never been a good hand with a gun, darling. Besides, as you said, it'll be Corky who's coming."

"Have it your way. I guess this gives you a chance to talk to him about the deal."

He nodded. "Aye, that's true. It's a chance to lay all our cards on the table." His eyes narrowed. "Something's bothering you about this."

"If Ian didn't kill Caleb, Corky might've done it."

"Aye, that's so. Come to that, anyone in the O'Malleys might have."

"I want to trust him," she said.

"But you don't quite."

"No, I don't. How can I? You said they send your best friend to kill you."

"Not Corky," he said in tones of absolute certainty.

"That's what Evan would want you to think."

"That *is* what I think. And you'd best not be part of the conversation."

"The hell I won't be. He won't have a gun, he doesn't carry, but I know how good he is with a knife. He could kill you with your damn IV needle! I'm not leaving you alone with anyone from the O'Malleys. Damn it, Carlyle, this is your life we're talking about here!"

"Erin, darling. I need you to listen to me." He squeezed her hand. "I know what I'm talking about. I've survived in the Life almost two decades. Corky won't want to turn. I don't particularly like being a gangster, but he does. It's who he is. And he's no traitor. I may be the only lad who can talk him around, but I need to do it myself. Alone."

"Why? That's way too dangerous. What if he gets mad?"

"Oh, he'll be angry, I guarantee it. He'll feel blindsided and betrayed. That's why I need to show I trust him. And so do you."

"You trust him more than you should."

"That's as may be," he said, unmoved. "The point is, if this is to work, you don't have to trust him. But you must appear as if you do. Because he'll only do this for friendship, not under coercion. If he feels we're ganging up on him, it'll be all the worse. Don't you know, darling, if you want a lad to trust you, you first need to make a gesture of trust toward him?"

"I don't like it," she said stubbornly.

"You needn't like it," he replied. "But it's the only way to win Corky over, and I'm not dragging him down. Either we all come through this together, or it doesn't happen at all."

Erin stared at him, trying to think of a way to convince him. Arguments slipped away from her. Because he was right, damn it all. The only way to win Corky to their side was to take a chance on him, and the appearance of the thing was essential.

"Okay," she said slowly. "We'll do it your way. But I won't be far away, and if he screws you, God help him. I swear, I'll kill him with my bare hands."

A knock on the door startled both of them. Rolf barked and sprang to his feet, bristling. Erin spun and dropped a hand to the gun at her hip. The guard stood at the window and waved to her.

She opened the door a crack. "What is it?"

"Got a guy here with some flowers. Says his name's Corcoran. You said to let him in."

Erin glanced past the cop. She saw a pair of legs clad in expensive shoes and well-pressed slacks. Above them was a ridiculously oversized bouquet of exotic flowers, behind which, presumably, was the man in question.

"Corky?" she inquired, trying to see around the blooms.

"Aye, love, it's me," he said, his voice slightly muffled. "I don't want to be a bother, but I'd like to set these down somewhere. They're a mite heavy."

"Come on in," she said. But as he struggled to fit the massive arrangement through the doorway, she stood back with a hand still resting near her gun. She made sure no one else was in the hallway as the door closed behind him.

"Corky," Erin said, "look at the size of that thing you're holding. That's embarrassing."

"Aye, I get that a lot," Corky said with a twinkle in his eye, gingerly depositing the flowers next to the bed. "I'm thinking Evan's trying to say something. In my defense, all I've done was pick up the order. I swear, I don't even know what half these pretties are called. You know why they have flowers at funerals, don't you, love?"

"Because they're pretty," she said.

"To cover up the smell of the dead fellow," he said, grinning. "What words can I say in the memory of Morton Carlyle, the dearest mate a lad could ever wish for? He was like a brother to me. The things we shared, I can't even begin to relate, and oughtn't, for there's a lady present..."

"I'm lying right here, Corky," Carlyle said.

"Are you?" Corky asked, looking at him in mock surprise. "God, but you gave me a fright! I thought you were a ghost!"

"Not just yet," Carlyle said.

The two men smiled at each other. Carlyle offered his hand, which Corky took in a warm grip.

"I'm never leaving this bloody town again," Corky said. "Look what happens when I do."

"It's not the leaving that's the trouble, I've found. It's the coming back." He paused. "We've some things to discuss, you and I."

Corky glanced at Erin and back at Carlyle. "Well, all right, if you insist. I understand if you can't fulfill your proper duties toward this fine lass in your present condition, and I'll be glad to provide whatever services she requires."

"That wasn't precisely what I was thinking," Carlyle said. "Listen, lad. What I'm going to ask you is important, and for your ears only. If you'd give us some privacy, darling?"

"Sure," Erin said, trying to sound casual. "I'll just wait outside. Rolf, *komm!*"

She and her K-9 stepped into the hall. Erin made herself act nonchalant. She didn't look through the window, didn't put her ear to the door.

"You think it's a good idea leaving that guy in there with him?" the guard asked, craning his neck to take a look.

"I don't know if anything's a good idea where that man's concerned," she said, meaning Corky. "You just have to do the best you can."

Chapter 8

Waiting was an essential part of police work, whether doing a stakeout, looking for lab results, or hoping people would return phone calls. Erin had never liked it or gotten completely used to it. She drummed her fingers against her leg and wondered whether she'd have the chance to do anything if Corky went for Carlyle.

She probably wouldn't. She'd seen Corky use a knife. He could move faster than any man she'd ever met. If he decided to kill Carlyle, there was no human way she could stop him.

Why had she agreed to this crazy plan? She looked down at Rolf, maybe hoping for inspiration, but all she saw in his serious eyes was bottomless trust, a trust she didn't feel she deserved.

"What's this all about, anyway?" the guard asked.

"That's need to know," she replied.

"Of course it is," he muttered. "I hate babysitting details."

"Hey, it could be worse," she said. "You could be guarding a politician."

He snorted. "Yeah, or a celebrity."

Erin checked the time. She should be at work by now. She opened her phone and texted Webb that she'd be a little late coming in. Hopefully he wouldn't be too upset. Not that anything she could do now would be likely to make him or Vic angrier than they already were.

Webb's answer came in a few moments. It said, "Looking forward to seeing you once you free up your busy schedule."

"And there I was, afraid he'd be mad," she said under her breath.

She couldn't hear anything from the room. No shouting or screaming was probably a good sign. She kept waiting and trying not to worry. Time crawled by.

Erin jumped and stifled a cry. Something cold and wet had poked her in the hand. She looked down and saw Rolf. He'd nudged her with his snout. He looked a little worried about her. She scratched him behind the ears and was rewarded with a tail wag.

The door swung open. Erin and the other cop spun toward the doorway. Corky stood there. For a second, Erin couldn't think what was wrong with his face. Then she realized he wasn't smiling. His bright green eyes, which usually held a mischievous sparkle, were dark and thoughtful.

Erin couldn't help herself. She looked past him toward the hospital bed, just to make sure. Carlyle was lying there, pale and tired, but definitely still breathing. She saw no bloodstains on the bedsheets.

"All done?" the guard asked Corky.

Corky nodded.

"Then get outta here," the cop said. "This ain't a zoo and it ain't a museum."

Carlyle made eye contact with Erin through the doorway. He cocked his head in a small but significant motion, indicating she should stick with Corky. Then he nodded slightly, lay back, and closed his eyes. He was clearly exhausted.

Corky had walked right past Erin without seeming to notice her, another unprecedented thing. She went after him, catching up partway toward the exit.

"You okay?" she asked him.

He nodded.

"The hell you are," she said. "Since when do you not have a smartass comeback?"

Corky's hands moved so fast she almost didn't see them. He grabbed her shoulders and spun her to face him.

"What the hell more do you want from me? Haven't you done enough?"

"I didn't have a choice!" she hissed, trying to keep her voice down. "But Carlyle did, and so do you!"

"No, I bloody well don't!" he snapped, but she was gratified to hear him using a fierce whisper. "If you think I'd ever go against my best mate, you're out of your head!"

"Then what are you complaining about?" she retorted. She saw an open examination room on her right and pulled him through the doorway, swinging the door shut with her foot behind them. Rolf managed to scamper through, narrowly escaping a pinched tail.

"Are you going to cry over jerks like Mickey Connor?" she went on, wrenching free of his grip.

"That's not the point! You put Cars up to this! Isn't this what you wanted all along?"

"This was never the plan!" she said, more loudly than she should have.

They stared at one another. Then, irresistibly, a hint of his habitual smile dawned on Corky's face. "Something we can agree on," he said.

"I didn't mean to fall for him," Erin said softly. "It just happened, one thing at a time."

"I can't fault you for that," Corky said. "I love him myself. Not the same way, of course. You've a right dirty mind sometimes, has anyone ever told you that?"

"We were trying to keep it a secret," she said. "From my people."

"What, exactly, did you think was going to happen? Did you really think you'd get away with it?"

"*You're* asking me that?" she shot back. "When did you become a long-term planner?"

"Fair enough, love. But you're supposed to be the sensible one. You were so sensible you wouldn't sleep with me, remember?"

"That's kind of a low bar to clear, Corky."

He made a pained expression. "Ouch."

"Look," she said. "I didn't want to involve you, either. But Carlyle insisted. Either you come in, or he won't go along with the operation."

"I ken what you're saying," he said. "Cars explained it all to me."

"Then you know we have to take down all of them," she said. "Evan and his whole crew. You're the only one he couldn't hand over. He loves you like a brother. He'd never go against you."

Corky nodded. "I suppose it was always going to go one way or the other. I'd just rather hoped you'd come over to our side."

"Be a gangster?"

"It has its attractions, love. Money, freedom, fast cars, loud music..."

"Easy women and booze?"

"The lads are easy, too," he said, and his smile was bigger and more genuine now. "You could try it, love. Who knows? You might like it. More than I'd like the straight life, I fear."

"That's not who I am. It never was."

"Nay, I reckon not," he said. "But you ken how dangerous this will be?"

"Is that what's worrying you? The danger?"

He laughed out loud. "For me? Never. It's you I'm worrying about, and that lad lying back there with the extra hole in him. I've never worried what's going to happen to me. But this isn't what I came back from Mexico to do."

"What did you come back for?"

"You don't want to know, love."

"Try me."

He gave her a look. "You're really asking? To deal with the bastards who shot my best mate, of course."

"Corky? Where were you last night?" The question came automatically.

"Why are you asking me that? If you don't trust me, you shouldn't have brought me in on this wee dirty secret. And if you do trust me, that's no question to be asking."

"That's not an answer," she said.

"What if I gave you an answer you didn't want? What would you do? If something happens to me, how do you think it's going to go over with Cars? You think he'll forgive you for that?"

Erin didn't have an answer.

"That's what I thought," Corky said. "I'll be taking my leave now. We've both places to be, I'm thinking. I know where I stand. Perhaps you should be deciding that for yourself, aye? Am I your friend, or your bloody tool, or just another lad who's standing in your way?"

"I thought we were friends. But I thought that about some other guys, too, and I think maybe I was wrong."

He paused on his way to the door. "If friendship's such a scarce commodity, perhaps you should be taking a mite better care of it, love." Then he was gone.

Erin could have gone after him, but she didn't see the point. She was late for work, and besides, Corky clearly wanted to be left alone. She just had to do what Carlyle had said, and trust him.

But if friendship was scarce in Erin's life, trust was even scarcer.

* * *

She wasn't looking for a warm welcome at Precinct 8, so she wasn't disappointed. Vic and Webb were in Major Crimes, doing paperwork, when she arrived.

"Glad you could join us," Webb said sourly.

"Didn't notice you weren't here," Vic grunted.

"What's going on?" she asked.

"Writing up the Thompson arrest," Webb said. "We don't have a confession, but we hardly need one. We've got all kinds of evidence."

"Even the security footage from our own front door," Vic put in. "You can see Thompson and Carnahan getting into the same damn car, just a few hours before Carnahan gets whacked."

"So that's it?" Erin asked. "He's being charged?"

"As soon as we get everything squared away here," Webb said. "Then, assuming the judge doesn't grant bail, off he goes to Riker's Island to wait for trial."

"It's Judge Ferris," Vic added. "You think he'll give bail on a Murder One charge?"

"Stranger things have happened," Webb said.

"Yeah?" Vic challenged. "Name one."

"The Red Sox winning the '04 World Series," Webb said.

Vic thought that one over for a second. "Okay," he said. "I'll give you that, sir. But only 'cause I'm a Yankees fan, and the Sox can go straight to hell."

"Did we get Levine's report yet?" Erin asked.

"Not yet," Webb said. "Why don't you go down to the morgue and see how it's coming?"

"Yes, sir," she said, only too glad to get out from under Vic's glare. She and Rolf descended to Levine's domain. Maybe, if she was lucky, the Medical Examiner would have something that would point the blame away from Ian. Because if not, he was looking increasingly screwed.

Bodies didn't bother Erin; city cops got used to encountering death. But the smell of the morgue was something she could never quite accustom herself to. In spite of Rolf's sharp nose, the formaldehyde stench didn't seem to bother him, but Erin's own nose wrinkled when she went through the stainless-steel door.

There was Levine, as expected, standing over what was left of Caleb Carnahan. He was considerably the worse for wear since the last time Erin had seen him. Apparently Levine had recently finished the autopsy.

"Morning, Doc," Erin said.

"Correct," Levine said without looking up.

"Huh?"

"Nine twenty-five," Levine said. "Before noon. Therefore, morning."

"Right," Erin said. "What've you got on our stiff?"

"Cause of death matches initial external examination," Levine said. "The subject received two gunshot wounds from a single bullet which passed through the palm of the hand, shattered the middle metacarpal bone, and entered the cranium just above the nasal cavity. The bullet was already deformed and tumbling from contact with the hand, so the entrance wound is oblong. Death resulted from traumatic destruction of the brain and was instantaneous."

"And you're sure the bullet was the one we found in the wall behind him?"

"Blood and tissue on the bullet is a match for the subject," Levine confirmed.

"What about the bruising on his face?" Erin asked.

"The facial contusions were inflicted ante-mortem and were not life-threatening," Levine said. "I'm quite certain they were inflicted by human hands, clenched into fists."

"Any way you can tell whose hands did the damage?"

"I haven't been able to isolate any foreign skin cells," Levine said. "It's likely the assailant was wearing some form of hand prophylactic, probably thin gloves. The wound markings are not distinctive enough to match to a specific hand, but were inflicted by someone striking with great force."

"How much force?" Erin asked.

"At least twelve hundred pounds."

"Twelve hundred pounds?" Erin echoed. "That's like getting stomped on by a horse. People can punch that hard?"

"A study of professional boxers found heavyweight fighters could strike with thirteen hundred pounds of force," Levine said. "In 1985 a boxer named Frank Bruno did a lab test in which the scientists extrapolated his striking force to one thousand, four hundred twenty pounds, which would cause an acceleration of approximately fifty-three times the force of gravity to an opponent's skull."

"Ouch," Erin said. "But you're saying getting slugged didn't kill our guy?"

"He was hit in the face," Levine said. "The face is a good shock absorber. It's much more damaging to be struck on the sides, top, or back of the skull. His left cheekbone was fractured, however, as was his jaw. His nose was broken as well, but none of those injuries would have been life-threatening."

"Would they have knocked him unconscious?"

"Possibly. However, he was likely conscious at time of death."

"Right," Erin said. "Otherwise he wouldn't have thrown up his hand to take the bullet. How hard does a normal guy hit?"

"Define normal," said Levine, who wasn't normal under any definition Erin could think of.

"Let's say a pretty fit man, twenty or thirty, average height. A guy who works out regularly."

"That doesn't fit the median profile of an American male."

Erin managed not to roll her eyes. "Still, how much weight could a guy like that put into a swing?"

"Maybe five to seven hundred pounds of force, if he knows how to strike efficiently."

"So Carnahan was beaten up by somebody who was unusually big and strong?"

"And in all likelihood a trained fighter," Levine agreed.

"Was he drugged?"

"His bloodwork showed mild alcohol intoxication, a BAC of .03," Levine said. "Well under the legal limit. No other drugs in his system. Stomach contents indicate he'd eaten about three hours prior to death."

"What'd he eat?" Erin asked, glad she hadn't had the job of going through the dead man's guts.

"Cheeseburger and French fries."

"What restaurant?" Erin asked, half joking.

"I'm working on isolating the grease used to fry the potatoes," Levine said. "Unfortunately, I don't have a positive result yet. Would you mind having samples sent down from every restaurant in Manhattan that serves cheeseburgers?"

"Levine," Erin said. "Do you have any idea how many fast-food joints are in Manhattan?"

"No, I don't. If it's inconvenient, just try to get them to me later. I think I might publish a paper on it."

"Did Carnahan have any defensive wounds?" Erin asked, figuring it was time to change the subject.

"I found a heavy contusion on his left forearm," Levine said. "It appears he blocked one blow with that arm. This resulted in a hairline fracture of the ulna."

"This guy really got wrecked," Erin said. "Sounds like it wasn't much of a fight." That surprised her. Caleb had been a big man, a little out of shape but still strong. As a Mob security guy, he'd certainly have known how to fight.

"Got anything else for me, Doc?" she asked.

"I'll send up the report momentarily," Levine said. "Without the restaurant identification."

"Thanks," Erin said. As she took the elevator back up to Major Crimes, she found herself thinking of the one man she knew in the O'Malleys who had the physical strength and skill to deliver a beating like the one Levine had described.

"I think Mickey beat the crap out of him," Erin said to Rolf. "But why? And who told him to? Mickey's an enforcer. He doesn't go for someone unless someone higher up the ladder turns him loose. And Mickey doesn't like to carry a gun. So who shot Caleb?"

Chapter 9

"Ian Thompson didn't beat up Caleb Carnahan," Erin announced.

"What's your point?" Vic retorted. "I don't care what else he did besides put a bullet in that idiot's head."

"It's important," she insisted. "If Carnahan got in a fight right before he was shot, don't you think we should know about it?"

"How do you know Thompson isn't the one who beat Carnahan?" Webb asked.

"He's not big or strong enough."

"He's kind of a little guy," Vic agreed. "But he's also a badass. Dude used to be a Marine. I could take him, sure, but he could thrash your average street punk."

"Plus, he probably had Carnahan at gunpoint," Webb said.

"That doesn't matter," Erin said. She turned on Vic. "I just talked to Levine. The physics don't work. Have you ever broken a guy's jaw?"

He shrugged. "Not that I know of, but I snapped a mope's collarbone once, and I've broken a couple noses. Cracked another guy's ribs one time."

"Carnahan had two broken bones in his face, plus his nose, and a fractured forearm," she said. "From fists. How many guys do you know who can hit that hard?"

Webb said nothing.

Vic rolled his eyes. "He could've used brass knuckles."

"Those leave marks. You think Levine wouldn't have noticed?"

"Jesus Christ, Erin," Vic said. "What's got into you? I know you like the guy, but this is more than that. Are you actually working for the Mob now?"

"You want to see how hard a woman my size can punch, say that again," she growled. "And Thompson doesn't work for the O'Malleys, not directly."

"Says you," Vic muttered.

"I'm not saying anything here that a defense lawyer won't say at his trial," she said. "If you're serious about making a good case, we better have answers before then."

"O'Reilly's right," Webb said. "We need to know more about what happened. The timeline has too many gaps. Thompson hasn't exactly been helpful with his alibi."

Vic snorted. "By which you mean, he hasn't told us shit. Because he doesn't have an alibi. Because he killed Carnahan!"

"He'll talk to me," Erin said. "Let me try."

"He's lawyered up, O'Reilly," Webb said wearily. "You can't talk to him without that weasel Walsh looking over his shoulder the whole time."

"Then get Walsh down here," she said. "If he's got something that'll help him, his lawyer won't stop him from saying it."

"You're emotionally compromised," Webb said. "You can't look at this objectively."

"Why does that matter?" she shot back. "You'll be watching me the whole time. My emotional connection to Ian is what'll get him to talk to me. He didn't give you or Vic anything. You let Vic talk to Tatiana last year, and that worked."

"Okay, we'll try it," Webb said. Seeing Vic open his mouth to protest, the Lieutenant held up a hand. "And if you do anything to jeopardize this case, you'll be a meter maid in the Bronx by the end of the week."

"I'm not sure you can actually do that, sir," Erin said, relieved.

"Don't test me," Webb said.

*　　*　　*

Walsh took about half an hour to get to the precinct, which was pretty fast, considering. A suspicious person might wonder how Ian, on his limited salary, could afford such high-powered legal representation on such short notice.

Erin normally would have wondered exactly that, but she didn't have to. She knew Walsh was kept on permanent retainer by the O'Malleys, along with a couple of other experienced defense attorneys, for exactly this kind of situation.

Walsh came in wearing an expensive suit and an aura of invincibility. He was prepared to deflect or refuse to answer anything and everything, all while being paid a thousand dollars an hour. It was a solid wage in return for doing essentially nothing.

The detectives had already moved Ian into the interrogation room. Vic and Webb were next door, observing through the one-way mirror. Erin sat down opposite Walsh and Ian. It was unusual to be doing this solo, giving the suspect and his lawyer the psychological advantage of numbers, but that was part of Erin's gambit. Rolf, of course, wasn't allowed in interrogations. He was leashed to Erin's chair upstairs in Major Crimes, having a nap next to her desk.

"Thank you for coming in, Mr. Walsh," Erin said.

"My client won't be answering any questions regarding your department's outrageous accusations," Walsh said. "He is completely innocent of any wrongdoing."

"I agree," she said.

There was a second of silence. Walsh glanced at Ian, who maintained his usual quiet, neutral expression.

"Then I don't quite understand what any of us are doing here," Walsh said.

"I need Ian's help finding the guy who killed Caleb," she said.

"This is not how you people normally go about doing this," Walsh said. "If you're admitting to knowingly and deliberately arresting the wrong man—"

"I'm doing nothing of the sort," Erin interrupted. "I didn't arrest your client and I didn't charge him. I'm not in a position of authority here. I'm asking Ian to help me and to help himself at the same time. I don't know for sure what happened last night, but the way the evidence is stacking up, either he shot Caleb Carnahan, or someone really wants to make it look like he did."

Walsh sat back and folded his hands. The look on his face was one of polite disbelief. He'd probably honed it in courtrooms listening to opposition testimony. "Okay, Detective. What questions do you have? Remember, Mr. Thompson, you're under no obligation to reply, and I encourage you not to."

"I understand, sir," Ian said without taking his eyes off Erin.

"Ian, you keep pretty good track of your guns," she said. "You own two Beretta nine-millimeters, correct?"

"Don't answer that," Walsh said.

"Yes, ma'am," Ian said, ignoring his lawyer.

Walsh rubbed his temples and looked disgusted. Erin reflected that he'd recommended pointless obstruction. The gun permits were on file with the city and had been completely aboveboard and legal.

"Where do you keep them?" she asked.

"I usually carry one with me, ma'am. The other one stays in the gun locker at home."

"Which you keep locked?"

"Always."

"How could someone have gotten their hands on that gun?"

Ian shrugged. "With the key to the locker, ma'am, or by popping the lock."

"And no one else had a key?"

"No, ma'am."

"We've been over this ground already, Detective," Walsh said. "If you have nothing new, this interview is over."

"I know you talked to Evan O'Malley last night," Erin said. "Where did you meet him?"

"I don't think that's relevant, ma'am," Ian said.

"Okay," she said. "Let's just say you were in a meeting after you got out of lockup. How long were you there?"

"A couple of hours, ma'am. We got out at 1230 hours."

"We meaning you, Caleb Carnahan, and Mickey Connor?"

"Yes, ma'am."

Walsh closed his eyes, clearly wishing he was somewhere else, no matter what his hourly rate was.

"Was that the last time you saw Caleb?" Erin asked.

"No, ma'am. We went to a room and waited."

"For what?"

"They didn't tell me, ma'am."

"They were checking out your story," she guessed. "Looking for inconsistencies."

"That's speculation," Walsh said. "You're asking my client to extrapolate the thoughts and motives of people who aren't even here."

"When did they let you go?" Erin asked.

"About 1800 hours, ma'am."

"Six PM," Erin translated aloud. "Did you and Caleb talk about anything while you were waiting?"

"No, ma'am."

"Was anyone else in the room with you?"

"Yes, ma'am."

"Who?"

"I didn't know their names, ma'am. Two guys."

"Armed?"

"That's not relevant," Walsh said.

"Yes, ma'am," Ian said. "Handguns under their coats."

"You saw the guns?"

"Saw the bulges and the straps for the shoulder holsters, ma'am."

"Would they have let you leave?"

"Don't know, ma'am. I didn't ask."

"What do you think?"

"Speculation," Walsh said again.

"Didn't make tactical sense to try," Ian said.

"Caleb was there with you?" she asked, just to make absolutely sure.

"Yes, ma'am."

"Until six?"

"Yes, ma'am."

"When they let you go, what happened to Caleb?"

"He got in a car."

"What car?"

"Don't know, ma'am."

"What did it look like? Make? Model? Color?"

"Black. Chevy Suburban."

"Who else got in the car?"

"The two guys who'd been in the room with us."

"Did you go with them?"

"No, ma'am. I went home."

"How'd you get home?"

"Taxi."

"Did you pay by card?"

"No, ma'am. Cash."

"When did you learn your gun was missing?"

"As soon as I got there, ma'am."

"Do you always check your guns when you get home?"

"Yes, ma'am. And I needed to re-equip."

"What do you mean?"

"The police confiscated my sidearm after the incident, ma'am," Ian said, meaning the shooting at Erin's apartment. "I needed something else to carry. The situation was tactically fluid."

"Did you feel endangered?" she asked.

For the first time in the interview, Ian looked a little confused. "How do you mean, ma'am?"

"Did you feel that you needed to arm yourself in case someone was coming after you?"

"I always feel like that, ma'am."

Walsh very slowly put a hand over his face. "Mr. Thompson," he said softly, "will you please, for the love of God, stop talking?"

"What did you do then?" Erin asked.

"I had dinner," Ian said, ignoring his lawyer.

"What'd you eat?"

He shrugged. "Food."

"You don't remember?"

"Ma'am, I did my time in the Corps," he said. "It wasn't a good idea to pay too much attention to what we were eating. It was something frozen, out of a cardboard box. Hot pocket, I guess."

"Did you leave your apartment again that night?"

"Yes, ma'am."

"When?"

"When your squadmate arrested me."

"But you were there the whole evening until then? What were you doing?"

"That's not relevant—" Walsh began, making one last try.

"Cleaning and checking my other guns," Ian said matter-of-factly.

"We're done here," Walsh said, standing up.

"Just a second," Erin said. "Why check your guns, Ian?"

Ian looked at her like she'd just asked a stupid question. "Someone had been in the locker," he said. "I'm not going to trust a gun someone else might have handled without checking it."

"Why didn't you report the theft?" she asked.

"I'd just been arrested, ma'am. Would your people have believed me when I reported a firearm theft?"

"Is there anything else, Detective?" Walsh asked through his teeth.

"Did you kill Caleb Carnahan?" she asked Ian.

"No, ma'am, I didn't."

"That should do it for now," Erin said. "Thanks for your cooperation."

"Ma'am," Ian said.

Chapter 10

After returning Ian to lockup, Erin met Webb, Vic, and Rolf upstairs in Major Crimes. She wasn't sure what to expect.

"You told Thompson's lawyer you think he's innocent?" Vic exploded.

"You can say anything you want in an interrogation room," Webb reminded him. "Remember when she seduced a confession out of that serial killer? As long as it gets what we need, I don't care. But now we're not in interrogation anymore, O'Reilly. Do you really think he didn't do it?"

"He didn't do it," she said, thinking she was still in an interrogation, all right. Just not Ian's. "He doesn't talk much, but he's not a good liar."

"What was the point of that, anyway?" Vic asked.

"Evan O'Malley was trying to find out who was behind the hit attempt on Carlyle and me," she said. "He knew it was either Caleb or Ian."

"How do you figure that?" Webb asked.

"There was no other reason to keep the two of them all afternoon," she said. "He was checking their stories. That means

Evan didn't sign off on the hit. And Evan decided Ian was innocent."

"And Carnahan wasn't?" Webb prompted.

"The last anyone saw of him was getting loaded in a car with a couple of heavies," she said. "And then he turns up in a back alley, beat to hell with a bullet through the head. Yeah, I think Evan had him whacked. Which should convince you I'm not working for the damn O'Malleys, Vic."

"That doesn't make Thompson innocent," Webb pointed out. "If you're right, how do you know O'Malley didn't have him pull the trigger?"

"For the last time, sir, Ian doesn't work for Evan," she said. "He hardly knows the guy and he sure as hell doesn't trust him. He only takes orders from Carlyle."

Webb leaned forward. "What if O'Malley told Thompson that Carnahan betrayed Carlyle? You think he wouldn't be willing to kill in that situation?"

"We all know he's willing and able to kill," she said. "Who are we kidding? But when he does, he does it in a focused, deliberate way. He wouldn't just toss his gun in the nearest dumpster and run off. Besides, he got straight in the car after getting released from the station. I saw it myself. He was unarmed at the time. We know that for a fact. If he didn't go home in the meantime, how did he get to the pistol?"

"We only have his word he didn't go home," Webb said.

"We can check traffic cams and see where the car went," she said. "We can talk to people in his building. I want to go there anyway, take a look at the apartment."

"CSU already went over it," Vic said.

"I know. But I want to see for myself."

"Okay. I'll go with you."

Erin blinked. "What?"

"You got a problem with that?" He scowled.

"Depends. You going to accuse me of being a criminal again?"

"Depends. You gonna commit any crimes? I'm going along to make sure everything goes smooth and by the book."

"Because you're such a smooth, by-the-book cop," Erin said in a flat deadpan.

"Just don't kill each other," Webb said. "I don't need the headache, or the extra paperwork."

*   *   *

"So what's the deal, Vic?" Erin asked as she drove the Charger out of the garage. "Just couldn't resist the urge to yell at me some more?"

"It gonna do any good if I do?" he replied.

"They say the difference between advice and blame is timing," she said. "Advice is useful. Blame isn't."

"Morton Carlyle," he muttered. "Jesus. What do you see in that guy?"

"He's not who you think he is," she said.

"Oh, so he's not a gangster? Not former IRA? Not a bomb-maker?"

"No, he's all those things," she sighed. "But he's not a bad guy."

"I'm not gonna like him, no matter what you say. And that's not the point. Look, when I was seeing Anna, I didn't know she was working with the *vory*."

Vic was referring to the Russian Mafia who'd used Vic's girlfriend to set him up. "What would you have done if you'd known?" she asked.

"Shit, I don't know. But I wouldn't have kept it a secret from my squad. Look, if you didn't feel guilty about this, we'd have known about it. So don't pretend you didn't know it was wrong."

"It was an accident, Vic."

"Oh, right, you tripped and fell into his bed. Of course."

"You know something, Vic? You are so full of macho bullshit sometimes. I have three brothers, so I recognize it. You guys think it's always about the sex."

"Here's where you tell me he's a great conversationalist? Listens to you? Understands you? He's a sensitive twenty-first century kind of guy?"

"I'm beginning to understand why you're still single," she said. "There's nothing I can say that'll convince you, so why bother?"

"Because I'd like to understand what made one of the smartest street cops I know do something so goddamn stupid!"

"If that's a compliment, you suck at them."

"It wasn't."

"I haven't done a single thing that compromises the Department," she said.

"Yeah? Is that what you told Internal Affairs?"

"What I told them is none of your business."

"Isn't it? I think maybe it is. If I'm supposed to trust you."

"I've still got your back, Vic. Whether you like it or not."

"Are you working for them?"

"For who?"

"Internal Affairs. Was that the deal they offered you? You looking over our shoulders now?"

Erin bristled. "I don't spy on my own side."

"Then what was the deal? What'd Keane make you do?"

She hesitated.

"I knew it!" Vic said. "He's got something on you, so now he owns you. Jesus, our own guys are as bad as the Mob sometimes. There's no way you would've been cleared so fast unless something was going on behind the scenes. I'm just surprised Captain Holliday's in on it. I always thought he was a straight shooter."

"Vic, you're jumping at shadows. Keep this up and you'll be seeing bad guys everywhere."

"Open your eyes, Erin. Bad guys *are* everywhere. That's the way the world works. How'd you get to be a detective? You're way too optimistic. Not to mention how you're vaulting up the promotion ladder."

"Is that what's eating you? That I made Detective Second Grade before you did?"

"Shit, Erin, you think I'm *jealous*? This isn't about me. I'm worried about you!"

"Worried? I thought you were pissed."

"I am. What, didn't your dad ever get pissed at you when you were out late? You think that was because he didn't care?"

"So you're my dad now?"

"Why are you mad at me? I'm not the one who did any-thing!"

"I'm only mad because you're mad!"

They glared at each other for a second. Then Vic snapped, "Eyes on the road!"

Erin returned her attention to her front windshield and jammed on the brakes, narrowly avoiding rear-ending a panel truck. They sat there, catching their breath and waiting for the light to change.

"We sound like an old married couple," she muttered. "Look, Vic, what can I say? I'm sorry. I could've handled this whole thing better, and I should've. If it's any comfort, my dad feels the same way you do."

"He's a retired cop, isn't he?"

"Yeah. And he knows Carlyle. From his time on the Job."

Vic whistled softly. "He ever arrest him?"

"No, Carlyle's never been arrested in New York."

"Oh, right. I knew that." Vic worked his jaw as if he was chewing a particularly tough mouthful of something. "So, this is a real thing? You in love with this guy?"

"Yeah, I am." She didn't look at him as she said it.

"Shit," he said. "You're screwed. You know that?"

"Tell me something I don't know."

"But you've gotta think about this, Erin. Just 'cause you love him don't mean he loves you back. He's using you."

"He was at the start. We were both using each other. But that's not what it is anymore."

"Is that what you told Keane? I'm having a hard time picturing him giving you a pass because of true love. I don't think that bastard's ever loved anyone or anything in his life."

"He's a cold, ambitious son of a bitch," she said. "But I told him the truth."

"I bet that surprised him," Vic said. "It always surprises cops when people are honest. Look, Erin, I'm pissed, okay? That's not gonna change. You screwed with the Department and you screwed with Webb and you screwed with me, and I can't forget that. But tell you what, just try to tell me the truth from here on out. Okay?"

"I won't lie to you," she promised. "Would you feel better if you took a swing at me?"

He thought it over. "Maybe."

"When this case is over, I'll give you a free shot."

"You crazy? I hit you, I could break you right in half. I'm, like, twice your size."

"I'll take my chances, steroid boy."

"I'll have you know, these muscles are a hundred percent natural." He flexed his shoulders and cracked his neck.

"That just means they're twice as expensive in the produce aisle."

And Erin felt a little better, because Vic couldn't help smiling just a bit.

*   *   *

They got the landlord to let them into Ian's apartment. He stayed in the hallway while they ducked around the police tape. As far as taped-off scenes went, it was very orderly. Ian had very little furniture and almost no decorations. A table from IKEA, a cheap-looking two-seater sofa, a single bookshelf, a TV, and a floor lamp were the only things in the living room. The kitchen was spartan and the dining room had a card table and two folding metal chairs.

"Looks like he never really moved in," Erin said quietly. Then she called to the landlord, "How long has he been here?"

"Just about two years," he replied. "Never had any problems with him."

Erin put on a pair of disposable gloves. Vic followed suit. They stood in the entryway, taking in the scene.

"We found a go-bag in the front closet," Vic said. "Two changes of clothes, a gift card for the Greyhound bus line. Seriously, who buys a bus gift card? And he had a storage locker key with the number filed off and five thousand cash. Dunno what the key opens. I'm guessing it's a locker at the bus depot."

"I can see why you think he's suspicious," she said, peering into the aforementioned closet. It was only half full. She saw an assortment of coats, shoes, and boots, all neatly arranged.

She looked at Rolf, who stared back expectantly.

"Rolf. *Such!*" she ordered. The Shepherd began snuffling enthusiastically, tail wagging. He was looking for people or explosives. If he found a person, he'd scratch and whine. If he found a bomb, he'd sit perfectly still and stare at it. His Bavarian trainers had realized it was best to teach him not to paw at anything that might explode.

"Erin, CSU searched the place already," Vic said.

"He might have a stash somewhere," she said.

But Rolf didn't turn up anything interesting. He led them to the bedroom and sniffed with interest at the gun locker, but it was open and empty.

"CSU carted off all the guns," Vic explained.

Erin glanced around the room. The bed was a simple twin size, one pillow and a blanket that looked like military surplus. She'd half expected a sleeping bag on the floor. She saw a dresser and a nightstand with a small lamp. That was it. No photographs, no flowers, nothing to liven the place up.

The bedroom closet held clothes, including a full set of Marine uniforms in clear plastic garment bags that didn't look to have been taken out or worn in quite a while.

"You could bounce a quarter off the sheet," Vic observed. "I guess after they drill bed-making into a guy in boot camp, he never forgets. He was awake when we came for him. Looks like he never went to bed."

Erin nodded and crouched next to the gun locker. It had a simple, sturdy-looking lock, but was standing open and empty. "Did CSU check for tampering?" she asked.

"I think so," he said. "But it's hard to tell." Both of them knew a skilled thief could pick a lock without leaving much evidence, but there might be scratches on the tumblers.

Erin looked closer at the lock. "Doesn't look like they took it apart," she said. She reached into her hip pocket for her Swiss army knife.

"Here, let me," he said.

"I can handle a screwdriver," she said, tackling the lock from the back. In a few minutes she had it apart. Rolf licked his chops and lay down next to his partner, nose twitching at the familiar scents of oil, steel, and gunpowder.

"Well?" Vic asked, looking over her shoulder.

"Have a look," she said.

The two detectives got as close as they could to the mechanism. Rolf nosed in alongside Erin and got elbowed back.

"CSU didn't check it," Vic said quietly. "Those stupid sons of bitches."

Erin nodded. The mark were plain to see. They'd both worked Patrol and responded to plenty of break-ins.

"Looks like the lock got raked," she said, meaning a pick had been moved up and down against the lock's components to simulate several possible positions for the tumblers. It was a quick-and-dirty way to open a simple lock.

"He should've had a keypad instead of an old-style lock," Vic said.

"He's got a Fox on the door," Erin reminded him. "Those things are solid. You're lucky he opened the door for you, or you'd have needed a sledgehammer." The Fox was a heavy-duty police lock which engaged a steel crossbar. To get through one of those usually required knocking the whole door out of its frame, and she'd seen the frame on the way in. Someone had done a custom job there, reinforcing the whole door.

Vic looked at Erin. She looked back.

"He could've tampered with the lock himself, I guess," she said at last. "To give the impression someone had broken in and stolen a gun."

"Cut the reverse psychology," Vic said. "You know as well as I do how crazy that sounds. Come on. If he'd thought we'd trace the gun back to him, he'd have just used another gun. One that wasn't registered in his name. It's not like he couldn't have found one."

"So where's that leave us?" she asked, knowing the answer but needing him to say it. Vic was a damn good cop when he used his head and stopped just reacting.

"It doesn't make sense," he admitted. "Either someone broke into this locker earlier, doing something unrelated, or Thompson was telling the truth and someone jacked his piece. But they only took the one gun, which also makes no friggin' sense. We found hundreds of dollars' worth of firepower in here when we busted him. Crooks don't just leave all that iron lying around."

"So it wasn't a normal burglary," she said. "And the front door lock showed no signs of tampering?"

"It looked fine to me," Vic said. "And there wasn't anything in the CSU report. But I guess we better look again. I still can't believe they missed something like this. I'm gonna hang that evidence tech on our bulletin board by his balls."

"They were looking at this as a suspect's residence, not a crime scene," she said.

Vic sighed. "Go on, say it already."

"Say what?"

"'I told you so.'"

"Will that make you happy?"

"Do I look happy?"

"You never look happy."

"That's not true."

"You rarely look happy."

"Hey, for a Russian, that makes me a comedian. But you're right, damn it. The only reason to take just the one gun, and then leave it at the crime scene, is to make us look at Thompson for the shooting. Which means it wasn't Thompson. Probably."

Erin nodded, trying not to show the enormous relief inside her.

"So who the hell was it?" he demanded.

"How am I supposed to know that?" she retorted.

"You knew everything else about this damn mess. Who was out to get Thompson? And Carnahan, come to think of it?"

"Two birds, one stone," she agreed. "I've got one suspect. But he doesn't quite fit either."

"Of course, Thompson might've had an accomplice..." Vic said, another thought hitting him. "Maybe the accomplice decided to screw him."

"Maybe, but he's always struck me as a loner," she said. "Remember his alibi?"

"At home, alone, cleaning his guns. I think that's the worst alibi I've ever heard. So, who's your suspect?"

Erin hesitated. Now she was right up against it. She wasn't supposed to bring any extra heat down on the O'Malleys. To do so would jeopardize her undercover assignment and put Carlyle's life, along with her own, in danger. But Mickey Connor was the only person she could think of who had the strength and skill with his fists to beat Caleb that way, he disliked Carlyle, and he loathed Erin.

"What's the problem?" Vic asked. His eyes narrowed. "Jesus, it's not Carlyle, is it?"

"No, Vic, it's not Carlyle," she said. "Thompson's alibi may be crap, but Carlyle's is rock solid. He's lying in a hospital bed missing a chunk of his guts. If he tried to leave, a bunch of alarms would go off and nurses would be all over him. I checked on him this morning. He's still there."

"Okay, one of Carlyle's buddies, then," Vic said. "That redheaded guy who hangs out with him, maybe? What's his name, Corcoran?"

"Corky's not strong enough to smash Caleb's face that badly," Erin said. "Besides, he never uses a gun. I don't think he's a very good shot. But he'd certainly have motive."

"It's not like Carnahan got hit from six blocks away," Vic said. "Our guy pretty much shoved the muzzle in his face. You saw the powder burns on his hand. He was probably touching the gun when it went off."

"Which is another reason it wasn't Ian," Erin said. "He's a sniper, remember? He really could hit his target from six blocks away."

"You can stop harping on that," Vic said. "Okay, I believe you. Thompson didn't shoot Carnahan. Why won't you tell me who did?"

"I'm not sure it was him," she said.

"So what? That's why we call them suspects, Erin. Once we're sure, we upgrade them to perps."

"There might be some... jurisdictional friction," she said, choosing her words carefully.

"Oh, no," Vic groaned, slapping his forehead. "I knew it. I just knew it. The only way this could get worse was to get the Feds involved. This guy under a RICO investigation or something?"

"Something like that," she said. "Look, it's not something we should be talking about."

"So what are we supposed to do? Tell you what, there's one thing we can do here."

"What's that?"

He smiled grimly and lowered his voice. "It would've taken a battering ram or the right key to get through this guy's front door. The door was still standing when we got here, so that means the gun thief had a key. Thompson says no one else had a key, so that means the landlord. Let's find out what he knows."

"You think he'll talk?" Erin asked.

"He'll talk to me. I'm gonna squeeze him until something I like comes out. And he's standing right outside. I'm gonna enjoy this."

Chapter 11

Compared to the average New Yorker, Ian Thompson's landlord was a big, tough-looking guy. Compared to Vic, he was a harmless, balding, overweight slob.

"C'mon in here for a second," Vic said.

"Whaddaya want?" the landlord growled.

"Whaddaya got?" Vic shot back, grabbing the guy by the shirtfront and hauling him into Ian's living room.

"Hey!" the man protested. "You can't just do that!"

The big Russian leaned in, still holding the landlord's shirt, making the guy bend backward to try to get away from him.

"I've just got one question and then we'll get out of your hair," Vic said. "What's left of it."

"Okay. Geez. Is this about the creep who lives here?"

"He giving you problems?" Erin asked. "You said he wasn't any trouble."

"Well, no." The man tried to shuffle sideways to get out from under Vic, but Vic wasn't having any of it and put an arm out on either side, gripping the edge of the desk. "He always pays his rent on time, always in cash. He always talks real polite."

"So why did you call him a creep?" she pressed.

"Those eyes, lady. You ever see him? They just go all flat and dead, like somebody turned off the lights inside his head. And he looks right through you. Look, I know you people took him away, and that's fine with me. I don't want no trouble. I don't know what he did, and I don't wanna know, okay? Forget about it. I'm done with him."

"I'm gonna ask you my question now," Vic said. "And I need you to pay attention to me. I got your attention?"

"Yeah, buddy."

"Look at me."

The landlord didn't want to meet Vic's eyes and Erin could hardly blame him. Vic's face was alarming at the best of times, and facing his scowl less than six inches away would unsettle almost anyone. But Vic, impulsive as he was, could be patient. He just stood there until the man, flinching a little, looked him in the face.

"Who'd you give the key to Thompson's apartment to?"

Erin knew why Vic had wanted the landlord looking at him. That way, when the man's eyes slid off to the side, it was really obvious he was being shifty.

"I dunno what you're talking about," he muttered.

Vic sighed and shook his head in mock sadness. "You know, buddy, when I was first working Patrol, I used to like it when guys gave me the runaround. It was kinda fun sorting out the bullshit from the truth. Because everybody lies to cops, did you know that? Even if they got nothing to hide. It's like they've all got this guilty conscience and the cop's gonna know if they break the speed limit, or cheat on their wife, or surf for porn when they're supposed to be working. Do you surf for porn? Am I gonna find dirty pics on your computer downstairs?"

"Huh? What? No!"

"I don't care if you got porn on that computer or not," Vic snapped. "I'm not the dick police. Focus. Nowadays, it just pisses me off when people lie, because it's wasting my goddamn time. Stop wasting my time, numbnuts, and answer the question."

Erin stifled a laugh. She knew Vic well enough to know he was mostly just messing with the guy, but the landlord clearly didn't know that. She tried to look stern and serious so she didn't undermine the other detective.

"I don't know," the man said weakly.

"Did you forget the question?" Vic demanded. "You gonna ask me to repeat myself? 'Cause I'm having a bad day and I don't like repeating myself. But I tell you what, I'll cut you some slack. Here's the question again. Who. Did. You. Give. The. Key. To?"

"Nobody," the landlord whispered.

"Then you got the key right here on-site? In your office?" Vic asked.

The landlord nodded.

"And if we check that key for fingerprints and DNA, it's only gonna have yours? Cause you didn't give the key to anybody else?"

The man looked sidelong again. "Look, buddy," he began.

"I'm not your buddy," Vic snarled. "Who got the goddamn key?"

"You're not in any trouble here," Erin said quietly. "Not yet. Just give us what we need and we're gone."

"You don't understand," the landlord said, looking her way as if she might save him from Vic. "I can't tell you."

"Why not?" she asked.

"He said he'd... kill me."

Vic glanced at Erin.

"So you did give the key to a guy," she said.

"What'd he look like?" Vic demanded.

But the landlord had gone as far as he meant to. He turned to Erin. "Look, lady, you said I wasn't in any trouble. Am I being accused of something?"

"Not at this time," she said. "But if Mr. Thompson chooses to press charges for criminal trespass and burglary, you'll be an accomplice."

"Hey, that's not true," he said. "This is my place, right? I own these apartments. I can go in any time I want, and so can my desig... my desig... the guy I choose."

"All that, and he's got a law degree, too," Vic said in disgust. "That's not saving you from a criminal complaint, punk. Not to mention you're going on the hook for Murder One."

"Murder?"

"Yeah, that's what it's called when somebody gets killed."

"I didn't kill anybody!"

"Doesn't matter," Vic said relentlessly. "If you helped the guy get the gun, you're an accessory."

The landlord was definitely sweating now. Erin saw him starting to crack. Normally she would have been happy about that, but if he identified the wrong guy, which in this case was the right guy, it would make her life that much harder. She had no idea what to do about it.

"He was a big guy," the landlord said.

"Big like me?" Vic asked.

"Bigger. Like, huge. Scariest guy I ever saw."

"Could you ID him in a lineup?"

The landlord shook his head vigorously. "I hope I never see him again. And I'm not picking nobody out of no lineup."

"Okay, that's it," Vic said and pulled out his handcuffs. "You're going down."

Erin put a hand on Vic's arm. "Don't," she said.

"Giving me an order?" Vic asked in a dangerously quiet voice. "You sure you want to do that now? For this?"

"Please," she said. "Trust me."

Vic scowled at her and stared into her eyes for a long moment. Then he turned back to the man.

"Your lucky day," Vic said to the man. "But tomorrow might not be so lucky. I think I'll come back sometime. You won't see me coming. You'll just look up one day and I'll be there. Smiling."

*   *   *

"Okay, Erin, what gives?" Vic demanded. They were back in Erin's Charger, on their way back to the Eightball.

"What?" she replied.

"First you insist Thompson's not the guy we want. Okay, fine, he's a killer, but he didn't kill this guy, so we don't nail him for it. I'm with you so far. But now you're trying not to find the guy who did kill our boy? Are you *trying* to leave this case unsolved?"

Erin said nothing.

"It can't be just 'cause the guy's an O'Malley," Vic went on. "Because we've busted O'Malleys before. And you already knew what this guy was gonna look like, because you already had a suspect, and that weasel back there practically confirmed it. It's all over your face. You know who killed Carnahan."

"I don't know who pulled the trigger," Erin said, which was technically true.

"But you know who swiped Thompson's gun and roughed Carnahan up. You know who's behind this."

Again, Erin said nothing.

"Is it because of the Feds? Because you never used to care what they thought. So they've got a RICO case going? Screw 'em. They'd swipe our case out from under us if they felt like it, so why not do the same to them? And how'd you know about the Feds anyway? Did Carlyle tip you off?"

Erin concentrated on her driving and tried to think.

"Okay," Vic said. "You're not gonna tell me. Is it because you don't trust me? Because I'd like to think I've earned a little trust from you."

"Have I earned any from you?" she shot back. "All the cases, all the fights we've been in together?"

"Yeah, you did. But you burned a lot of that to the ground with this whole Carlyle thing. So don't come crying to me about how I don't trust you. No, you're keeping something else back. And it's not because of me. It's because of..."

Vic trailed off and Erin knew he was thinking hard. Vic was smarter than he looked, as plenty of crooks had found out the hard way. She wondered whether he had enough pieces to put the puzzle together.

"It's either Keane or Holliday," Vic said suddenly, when they were only a block from the Eightball. "Gotta be. Which one?"

"Vic, I'm not a mind-reader. What the hell are you talking about?"

"One of them is running something and it's getting in the way of the case," he said. "They must've told you about it when you were locked up with them. And you're helping them. That's your price, it's why they didn't kick you off the Force."

"You know how that sounds?" she asked.

"Paranoid?" he replied. "Crazy? True?"

"Okay, Vic, let's suppose for a second you're not smoking paint chips," she said. "And let's suppose you're right. *If* that was true, and I was in on some sort of secret operation for the Captain..."

"Or Keane," Vic put in.

"Yeah, or him. If that was true, do you really think I'd be in any position to say a single word about it to anybody else? Even someone else on my squad? Because while we're being paranoid, how likely do you think it is that Evan O'Malley's got a source right here in the NYPD, feeding him everything we've got on his people?"

That shut Vic up long enough for Erin to park the car and unload Rolf. The Russian was particularly quiet and thoughtful on the elevator ride up to Major Crimes. Erin didn't know if that was good or bad, but she did know Vic was going to be a problem, a different one than he had been.

*   *   *

It was midafternoon by the time Erin, Vic, and Rolf walked into Major Crimes. Webb was at his desk, a cup of coffee at his elbow, a copy of the Times in front of him. The office was otherwise deserted. Even the whiteboard on which they charted cases was blank.

"Sir?" Erin asked. "What happened to the murder board?"

"Oh, I had the boys downstairs box up the stuff," Webb said, his head still hidden behind the paper. "The DA's office has charged Thompson, so it's off our plate. If you found anything at Thompson's place to add to the file, you can take it down and log it into Evidence."

"Wait a minute," Erin said. "You're saying the case is—"

"Closed, O'Reilly," he said. "Good quick work. Good work by your K-9, too. If he hadn't sniffed out that gun, it might not have been such a slam-dunk."

Erin looked at Vic. Vic looked at Erin.

"Little problem here, sir," Vic said.

Webb very slowly folded his newspaper and placed it on his desk. "Define 'little.'"

"Where's Ian?" Erin asked.

"On his way to Riker's Island," Webb said. "Prisoner Transport picked him up right after you left. Don't change the subject. What's the problem?"

"He's not our guy," Erin and Vic said in near-perfect unison.

Webb blinked. "Did you two rehearse this? Is this a prank? Have you been setting me up the last couple of days?"

"No, sir," Erin said.

"No, sir," Vic said. "I'm still pissed at her. But we're right. I mean, she was right to begin with."

"You're saying Thompson's innocent?" Webb asked. He took a pack of cigarettes out of his pocket, shook one into his hand and looked at it, clearly wishing New York's public buildings allowed smoking.

"Yes, sir," Erin said.

"You can prove it?"

"Don't have to prove innocence, sir," Erin said. "We have to prove guilt."

"The gun..." Webb began.

"Stolen from his locker right before the murder," she said. "The lock was raked. The thief got in by borrowing the landlord's apartment key."

"The landlord just gave a key to some random schmuck?" Webb asked, raising an eyebrow.

"The guy threatened to kill him," Vic said. "The landlord won't testify, he's scared shitless, but we got a rough description."

"Which is?"

"Bigger than me and scary as hell."

"That's not very specific," Webb said.

"Not that many guys are bigger than me," Vic said.

"Hair color?" Webb prompted. "Eyes? Weight? Ethnicity? Clothes? Anything?"

They shook their heads.

"That's not helpful," Webb sighed. "But Thompson was still one of the last to see Carnahan alive."

"We've got his alibi, sir," Erin said.

"Which is terrible," Webb added.

"But plausible," she said. "Sir, there's only one way this makes any sense, and that's a setup. He was framed."

"So you want me to call the District Attorney," Webb said, "and tell him that airtight, slam-dunk, guaranteed-conviction case he was so excited about is good to go, except that we think he might not be the guy?"

"He's not," Erin said in tones of complete certainty.

Webb looked at Vic.

Vic shrugged. "She sold me, sir. And I didn't want to believe her. How you think it's gonna play to a jury?"

"Like reasonable doubt," Webb said. "Okay, does either of you have any idea who this other guy is? The big scary guy?"

Vic looked at Erin, who tried to control her face as she answered.

"We can't be sure at this point. It's definitely a guy who's muscle for one of the rackets, but we'll need to look into Carnahan's situation a little more, find who his enemies were."

"So we're back to square one," Webb said. "Meanwhile, we keep bouncing Thompson in and out of lockup like a bunch of chumps. We'll be lucky if he doesn't file a harassment suit against the city. Okay, people. I'll talk to the Captain and he'll talk to the DA. He won't be happy, just like I'm not happy. We're the NYPD, not the Keystone Kops. Let's start acting like it. I want to know who killed Carnahan, and this time I want it to be the guy who actually did it."

"Mob hits are hard to solve," Erin began.

"If you wanted an easy job, why aren't you handing out traffic tickets in Podunk, Middle America?" Webb snapped. In that moment, Erin saw underneath her Lieutenant's weary exterior to the frustration and anger underneath. She wisely decided to stop pressing.

"Yes, sir," was all she said.

Webb stood up and started toward the Captain's office. Then he paused. His face softened a little.

"We'll get Thompson released as soon as we can, but there's protocols. It may take a little time. He'll probably be there overnight."

"I'm sure his lawyer will be real happy about that," Vic muttered.

Then it was back to work, but Erin didn't have a clue how to proceed. She knew who the shooter was, she was sure of it, but she couldn't think how to prove it. And even if she could, she was under specific orders not to. She sat at her computer, messing around in the database, killing time and thinking.

By five o' clock, the only conclusion she had was that she needed to talk to someone else, someone who knew more about this sort of thing than she did. That meant either Carlyle or Phil Stachowski. She didn't know Phil, didn't trust him, but he was her case officer, so she couldn't hide things like this from him. And what did it say about her situation that she felt safer trusting a professional criminal than another member of the NYPD?

* * *

After work, Erin started for home. She made it all the way up the stairs and was standing in front of her door, looking at the yellow police tape, by the time her brain caught up with her.

"Damn," she said quietly.

So she went back down the stairs, gave Rolf a quick walk around the neighborhood, and got back in her car to drive to Midtown.

On the plus side, a hot meal was waiting when she got there, baked lamb with crisp potato topping, and an apple pie baked by Mary O'Reilly for dessert. Her brother was working another evening shift, but Michelle, Anna, and Patrick were in good spirits. Erin's mom and dad were there too. Sean gave her a look when he asked how her day had gone, but she deflected with vague non-answers.

After supper, she had to submit to a long family conversation in the living room. Normally she would have enjoyed it, but Erin was distracted and fidgety. She kept thinking of Carlyle in the hospital and Ian locked up at Riker's Island. Ian would be fine, she told herself. But she couldn't quite convince herself of it. She should've done something more, fought harder for him. And there was the question of Mickey Connor. Not only was she certain he was behind Caleb's murder, that meant there was an excellent chance he'd been working with Caleb in the first place to set Erin and Carlyle up. Now he was snipping off his loose ends. And she'd be seeing Mickey in person tomorrow. How should she react? What would he say? What would he do?

Erin toyed briefly with the possibility of whipping out her Glock right there in Evan O'Malley's front hall and blowing a hole in Mickey's head. That would definitely convince them she was a gangster. On the other hand, it would mean she *was* a gangster. She decided that would be plan B. But she definitely needed to discuss things with Carlyle beforehand, and with Phil, too. Phil would help her prepare for the meeting as an undercover officer should. Carlyle knew the people and could give her tactical advice.

"Erin? Honey, are you all right?"

"Huh?" Erin blinked and looked at her mother. "Oh. Yeah. Just tired."

"Your father used to have the same look after a long shift," Mary said. "This job does take it out of you. Don't worry, I'm sure he's had days just like yours."

"Don't be so sure of that, Mary," Sean said quietly. "But you hang in there, kiddo. And let us know if you need anything. Anything at all." His mustache bristled slightly as he said it, and Erin had another image in her head. This one was of her walking into Evan O'Malley's front hall with Sean beside her and her dad blowing Mickey away. He might even do it if she asked nicely.

If family were the ones you went to when you needed backup in a gunfight, she supposed that made Vic her honorary brother. No wonder they were fighting.

Chapter 12

Erin's family conversation died down about nine o' clock. Visiting hours at Bellevue Hospital had ended at eight. Lacking the energy to fight her way through the hospital red tape, she decided to go see Carlyle in the morning. Fortunately, tomorrow was one of her days off, so she didn't need to shoehorn the visit into her work schedule again.

"I guess I'll turn in early," she said, standing up from the couch. "I might have a late night tomorrow."

"Good night, dear," Mary said, getting up to give her a hug.

Rolf sleepily stood and made a mighty stretch. Then he trailed his partner into the hall. Sean followed the two of them to the foot of the stairs. She turned, one hand on the bannister.

"What is it, Dad?"

"I'm worried, kiddo," he said in an undertone. "About you."

"I'm fine."

"You always say that. Sometimes it's true and sometimes it's not."

She shrugged. "It'll all be okay."

He laid a hand on her shoulder. "Seriously, kiddo. What's eating you?"

Erin decided to tell a bit of the truth. "My squad locked up the wrong guy," she said. "I'm trying to get it sorted out, but they already charged him. Now he's in Riker's overnight, and maybe longer."

He whistled. "That's rough. But it's part of the Job. You can't let things like that get to you. One night in a jail cell won't kill him."

"But I know the guy, Dad. He's... kind of a friend."

"Connected through your mutual acquaintance?" he asked very quietly.

She nodded.

"That's going to happen," he said. "Guys like that... they're not going to stop doing what they do just because of you."

"But he's innocent, Dad."

"Of everything? Or just of this one thing?"

"It's complicated."

"No, kiddo, it's not. It's really simple. There's the right thing to do and the wrong thing. Anyone tells you different, he's not looking out for you. And he's probably trying to sell you something."

Erin had no stomach for hashing this out with her father, not tonight. "I know, Dad," she said. She kissed his cheek, feeling the familiar scratchy tickle of his mustache. "Good night."

Sleep didn't come easy, and when it finally did, her dreams were lousy.

* * *

When Erin walked into his hospital room a little after eight, Carlyle looked surprisingly better than the last time she'd seen him. His cheeks had some color in them again, probably because of the tremendous amount of blood the doctors had pumped into him. His eyes were bright and clear. He was even propped slightly more upright in his adjustable hospital bed.

"Good morning, darling," he said. "Do come in. I'd stand to greet you, but..."

"That's okay," she said, smiling. "How're you feeling?"

"Grand. That's on account of the excellent narcotics your brother's people have been providing, but I'll not complain. Should he be looking for a sideline to his primary business, I know some lads he can talk to."

"I don't think Junior wants to moonlight as a drug pusher," she said, hoping and believing he was joking.

"But I'll be climbing the walls in here if this goes on much longer," he went on. "I know there's things happening on the street. I need to be out there, making moves of my own."

"You can't," she said. "Not yet."

"Perhaps not. But we need to be taking thought for ourselves, making our plans."

"I know. That's why I'm here."

"And here's me thinking it was on account of missing me."

Erin made a face. "Well, that too. Obviously."

"But we need to discuss our tactics, aye," he said. "And since I'm in no condition to do anything else, we'd best get down to business. First item, Ian. What's his situation?"

"He'll be fine," she said, taking a seat beside the bed and glancing back to make sure the door was closed and no one was eavesdropping. "I was able to prove someone broke into his place and stole the murder weapon." She explained what she and Vic had found at Ian's apartment.

Carlyle nodded. "Do you know who's behind it?"

"Mickey Connor."

He nodded again. "The only thing that surprises me is that Siobhan would have listened to him. She never liked that lad."

"Siobhan probably worked through Caleb," she said. "Maybe she didn't even know Mickey was behind it."

"And he may not be all the way at the bottom," Carlyle said thoughtfully. "Do you think he was operating with Evan's approval?"

"You know these guys better than I do," she said. "But I don't think so. According to Ian, Evan went to a lot of trouble to find out what was going on. If he was out to get you, he wouldn't have bothered. He would've already known. And," she added as the thought struck her, "he probably wouldn't have let Ian go free. We'd never have seen him again."

"That's an excellent point, darling. So Mickey's slipped his leash and made a play for the both of us. That tells us a couple of things."

"Which are?"

"Evan's losing his grip on the O'Malleys, and Mickey's well aware of it."

"Are either of those a good thing?"

He shook his head. "I fear we'll all be at one another's throats before all's said and done. You and I need to calm things down, if we're to see this through."

"I'll be hanging out with these guys tonight," she reminded him.

"Aye, that's our next item of business," he said. "There'll likely be some discussion of the situation. How do you want to come across?"

"That's easy. Evan told me to get Ian off the hook. I'm doing it. I just need to tell him I've proved Ian's innocence."

"You think that's easy?" he asked with a smile. "Evan doesn't care if the lad's innocent. In fact, it may be better if he thinks he's guilty."

"What?" Erin stared at him in disbelief. "You want me to tell Evan that Ian killed Caleb? Like hell I will!"

"Erin, darling," Carlyle said patiently. "We're talking about liars and criminals. Do you really care what they think, as long as it serves our purposes? As I've told you before, perception matters more than reality. Have you never bluffed over a weak hand of cards? If they perceive dear Ian being the sort of lad who'd kill for me on the street, that's all to the good. It makes the both of us look stronger."

"But Mickey knows Ian didn't do it."

"And he'll be telling Evan?" Carlyle asked with a knowing gleam in his eye.

"I guess not," she said. "Evan told me to get Ian off the hook, so he's not happy Ian got framed. Mickey setting Ian up won't sit well with his boss."

"Now you're understanding," he said with an approving nod. "You see, Erin, I'd rather like Ian to be my new head of security. But Evan won't like that, on account of Ian being outside the family, and not one of his own lads."

"But if Evan thinks he's murdered a guy for us," Erin said, "he'll think he's one of the team. Because he killed one of that team. You guys are all crazy, you know that?"

Carlyle smiled. "It's something of a cutthroat world, I'll grant. Sometimes quite literally."

"Then why not just tell Evan that Mickey set the whole thing up?" she suggested.

"Are you prepared to go to war with Mickey Connor?" Carlyle replied. "Right there, on the spot? Because that's what you'd be doing. And if you do it over a card table, with a few drinks in the lad, there's an excellent chance he'll kill you then and there."

"I could take him," she said.

"At close quarters? Alone? Darling, you'd not stand a chance. Nay, it's best for you to take credit for ordering the hit, and give Ian credit for carrying it out."

Erin tried to say something, but only an indignant splutter came out.

"Mickey will merely think you're being an opportunist, latching onto something he did," Carlyle continued. "He'll resent it, but it's nothing unusual in our world. It'll serve a double purpose. It'll make him think you're moving more into the Life and you're not onto him, and that'll buy credibility and time. Enough of both, perhaps, to conclude our business."

"Wait, back up. You want me to tell Evan I had Caleb killed?!"

"Lower your voice, darling. And you oughtn't to say it in so many words, of course. But aye, that's the impression you want to be creating. It's the best way to secure your position on the inside and avoid any further violence. I'd rather it not come to outright blows between Mickey's side and ours. Particularly when you're at Evan's house, by yourself."

"Corky would back me up," she said, a little sulkily.

"Aye, he would," Carlyle said with a chuckle. "The lad's been looking for an occasion to stick a pin in Mickey for some time now. But Corky's feeling a bit adrift after our conversation, I fear, and he may be a mite slow on the uptake. Regardless, if it comes to blows, chances are neither you nor he is walking out of that room. Evan will have his people there, as will Mickey, don't doubt it. It may be some consolation if the lads go down for murder once you're dead, but you'll be in no position to appreciate it."

"So I need to create the impression Ian's guilty," Erin said. "But I'm still getting him out of jail?"

"Precisely. That way you'll increase your value to Evan. If you can save lads of his that are guilty as sin, believe me, he'll like you the better for it. You and Ian both come out of this looking grand."

"Meaning I look crooked and he looks like a murderer."

"Erin, you're the one who came to me with the plan to take these bastards down," Carlyle said. "Didn't you know it'd come to this? Isn't this precisely the point?"

"Yeah, I guess. I just don't like it."

"If you did, darling, I'd be worried about you. But you'll do grand. They'll love you, except Mickey, and given that lad's already tried to have you killed at least once, I'd not lose any sleep over his good opinion."

"I feel so much better when you put it that way."

"I've spent the last two decades assuming some of these lads would kill me as soon as look at me," he said. "Trust me, you get accustomed to it."

"You guys are crazy," she said again. "But you're good at this."

"I've needed to be. That's how a lad makes the cut from being a young gangster to an older one, and it's why there's so few of us who make it."

"You're just full of comfort."

"Someone I loved tried to kill me earlier this week," he said. "It's diminished my optimism."

After a moment considering this, Erin said, "It could've gone down just like you say. I practically told Ian to take care of Caleb. Hell, maybe he was considering it. Maybe I'm better at this than I thought. Or worse."

"Erin. That's not what happened."

"Maybe not. But it nearly did."

"If you worry yourself about what almost happened, you'll be carrying a bit more weight than you need, darling."

"You're right," she said. "I've got plenty to worry about with what really did happen, and what's going to happen. At least I know what to say now."

"We've just one more item of business," he said.

"Good," she said. "This is my day off. I don't want to spend it sitting in meetings. What've we got?"

"Where are you sleeping?"

"At my brother's. Why? Not worried I'm with another guy, are you?"

He didn't smile at the weak joke. "I'm concerned for your safety. Is it secure?"

"It's a brownstone in Midtown. It's pretty solid. Sean and Shelley have good locks and an alarm system."

He nodded. "But I'd imagine the windows are plate glass and the door's not all that sturdy. I'd feel better if you were staying somewhere safer."

"Like where? Fort Knox?"

"You could stay at the Corner. In my flat."

Erin stared at him. "Did you just ask me to move in with you?"

"You needn't stay permanently, if you don't want. But for the duration of our precarious situation, it might be prudent. It'll be well-defended, especially once Ian's out on the street."

"I'll think about it."

"Erin?"

"Yeah?"

"I'd like you to be there. With me." He reached for her hand.

She took it and held it. "I know. But I don't know if I'm ready. Let's take this a day at a time, okay? Kind of a lot's been going on here. I don't want us to rush anything."

"I understand, darling." He sank back onto his pillow. Erin saw he was paler than he'd been when she'd gotten there, and he had lines and shadows around his eyes. He was in more pain than he'd been letting on.

"You'd better rest," she said. "I'm wearing you out."

"And not in the way I'd be wanting you to," he said with a weak smile. "Dear Lord, these drugs are making me sound like Corky."

"Maybe that's his secret," she said.

"Nay, he never touches the stuff. Be careful, darling. Please. Don't you go catching bullets. I can't in good conscience recommend it."

"Neither can Caleb." She bent over and kissed his forehead. "I love you."

*   *   *

That was her first meeting of the day. Her second was with Phil Stachowski. They met at a coffee shop halfway between their respective precincts, where hopefully no one would recognize them. They sat at a table outside the shop. Phil took his coffee with cream and sugar, Erin had hers with cream. All around them, the city of Manhattan went about its business and took no notice. Public places were often the best ones for clandestine meetings. They were almost impossible to bug and the background noise covered up anything sensitive they might say.

"How are you holding up so far?" he asked.

"I'm fine," she said, telling her favorite lie. "This is nothing I haven't done before."

"The main thing to remember is to see it for what it is," he said. "An opportunity. Just think what your alternate persona wants this to be and make sure that's how you come across."

"I know," she said, thinking of Carlyle's advice. "I think I've got it covered."

"Now, about the listening device," he began.

"No," she said flatly. "I'm not wearing a wire. Not tonight."

Phil sighed. "Erin, I know it's dangerous."

"Damn right it is. They find a wire on me, they'll kill me."

"I know that," he said patiently. "That's always what's on the line with a wire. Have they ever searched you?"

"No. But last card game I was there as Carlyle's guest. This time I'll be on my own. I don't know what precautions Evan might have in place. This is my chance to win their trust. I'm not wearing a damn wire, not this time."

"You're going to have to, sooner or later. Recorded testimony is one of the most powerful tools we have for getting convictions. It carries a lot of weight with juries. I've overseen fifteen major undercover operations, Erin. This is what works."

"I get that," she said. "And once I'm in, I'll be able to wear one. But things are too unsettled right now. I just don't have a good feeling about tonight."

"Do you think you're going into a dangerous situation?" he asked sharply.

Erin couldn't help laughing. "No shit."

Phil had to smile at that. "I meant, more dangerous than usual?"

"Carlyle and I think there's a power struggle going on in the O'Malleys," she explained. "Some of the people I'll be sitting down with are working against some of the other people." She paused and then thought, the hell with it. "I think one of them tried to have me killed already."

"I see," he said. "Remember, Erin, the case isn't worth your life. You said you've got a bad feeling about the wire. Is that just jitters?"

"How can I tell?"

"Examine the feeling. See if there's a reason."

Erin thought about it. "I think this is a test," she said. "If I pass, I'll be inside. More than I am now. But they'll be watching me extra closely tonight. This isn't the time to take any extra chances. I'll be on a tightrope even if everything goes the way it's supposed to."

"Okay. Listen to your intuition. You say no wire? No wire. But you and Carlyle are both going to be wearing them before this is over. We make them better than we used to. We're not talking about cramming a tape deck down the back of your pants. It's a risk, but it's a small one. We're not talking about drawing to an inside straight. The odds are in our favor."

"I know," she said. "But just trust me on this one, okay?"

"I do," he said with surprising earnestness. "And I'll have your back. Do you want a backup team standing by?"

"What, ESU guys with shotguns and assault rifles?" she asked, half joking.

"Exactly," he said, not joking at all.

"Not a good idea," she said. "We're meeting at one of Evan's homes. It's a swanky spot in Tribeca, across from Washington Market Park. We're not talking about some seedy drug den. If you have guys in tactical gear stacked up outside, people will notice. Besides, if things go sideways, it's not like they'll get there in time."

"And the more people we bring in, the greater the chance something leaks," he agreed. "But it's your life and your peace of mind, so it's your call."

"I'll take Rolf in with me," she said. "I think Evan will give me a pass on that. And at least one guy there is on our side."

He raised a skeptical eyebrow. "You're talking about Corcoran?"

She nodded.

"Are you sure of him?" Phil asked. "I've read his file. He's impulsive, flighty, unreliable."

"He's a handful," she agreed. "But if he's going to sell us out, we're already burned. Carlyle read him into the case yesterday.

He's not totally happy, but he's on board. And he loves Carlyle like a brother."

"Brothers betray each other," Phil said grimly. "I've seen it. It's great if he trusts you, Erin. But you can't trust him. It's not fair, but that's the way it is. Remember, you're always just one mistake from disaster, and it doesn't even need to be your mistake. And you don't want to trust too many folks in the NYPD, either. Keane wants to be Commissioner one day. Holliday wants to take down a dangerous gang. I want you to come home at the end of the night. That's my stake, but you don't even want to rely on me more than you have to. Being an undercover means flying solo."

"Copy that," she said. "Hey, this'll be easy. I'm halfway home already. Forget about it, Phil. I'm good to go."

"Glad to hear it, Erin. Anything else you need?"

"Yeah, a thousand bucks."

"Are you joking?"

"Actually, no. I need to buy in at the card table."

Phil smiled. "A thousand isn't much for this sort of thing. I have an emergency stash at my car. I can cover that. Just try not to lose it."

"That's the idea," she said. "But it's a card game. Anything could happen."

"Don't worry about that too much," he said. "Drop me a line afterward, no matter what time it is. I'd like to know you're still alive. I may not be able to sleep otherwise."

"Nobody's getting killed tonight," she said, hoping it was true.

Chapter 13

Erin wished she wasn't living out of a suitcase. Her clothing for the O'Malley get-together was an important tactical decision and her wardrobe was limited. She ended up having to ask Michelle's assistance. Her sister-in-law was a little taller than she was, and a little curvier, but some of her clothes could do in a pinch.

"What kind of party is this?" Michelle asked. They were in the walk-in closet in the master bedroom, sorting through clothing after dinner. Erin had spent the afternoon with family, which had been a little more awkward than usual. She was trying to get her head in the right place for dealing with mobsters.

"It's an evening event," Erin said. "Cocktails, card game, that sort of thing. Think James Bond."

"What effect are you looking for? Do you want to fade into the background, or do you want to knock their socks off? This red number here, I guarantee they won't be looking at your face."

"I bet they won't," Erin said, thinking it looked like about two-thirds of a slinky dress. "How do you fit into that?"

"After two kids, I probably don't anymore," Michelle laughed. "A little too much?"

"A little too little," Erin corrected. "I don't want that kind of attention, not from the guys I'll be hanging out with."

"Skirt or slacks?"

"Slacks." No way was Erin going into a potentially dangerous situation without pants.

"How about this?" Michelle suggested, holding up a teal silk blouse. "It fits me pretty tight, so it should go on you okay. That color works for you. Besides," she added with a wink. "If you change your mind about attracting attention, just pop the top two buttons."

"Shelley, for a stay-at-home mom, you've got a dirty mind." Erin started changing into the offered blouse.

"Who are these guys, anyway?" Michelle asked.

"Underworld contacts," Erin said, truthfully enough.

"That sounds exciting."

"That's one word for it."

"Do you need a wing-woman? I could tag along."

Erin blinked and tried to formulate a diplomatic answer. "No, Shelley, I don't think that's a good idea."

Michelle pouted. "I never go anywhere anymore."

"Trust me, Shelley, some of these guys are people you don't want to mess with."

"You're messing with them."

"It's my job."

"Okay. But I want some stories. Some juicy gossip."

"I can't comment on an ongoing investigation."

"You're no fun."

"Shelley, this isn't supposed to be fun. It's my job. If I do it right, nobody's going to get killed tonight."

"Are you joking?"

"Do I look like I'm joking?" Erin clipped her Glock to her hip and put her arms through the sleeves of a black leather jacket. "I'll probably be out late. Don't wait up."

*   *   *

She was carrying her gun, but she wasn't expecting to use it. She didn't bother with a bulletproof vest, either for her or for Rolf. The game had already begun. She wanted to appear assertive, confident, and dangerous. The gun was fine. The vest would have made her look weak.

She got lucky and found a parking place a short distance from Evan's apartment. Tribeca was a very upscale neighborhood, one of the most expensive in Manhattan. She knew this was just one of the places the O'Malley chief kept. He had a house in the Hamptons, where Erin had actually stayed for a few days earlier in the year, along with at least two other houses, and probably a good bit of other real estate. All of it was owned by shell companies and fronts.

The doorman in front of the apartment was immaculate in a dark green uniform with polished brass buttons and trim. He actually bowed slightly to her as he opened the door.

"Miss O'Reilly?" he asked politely.

"Yeah, that's me." She wondered how he'd recognized her and whether he was one of Evan's guys.

"Top floor, ma'am. You're expected."

Erin thanked him and tipped him a five, not knowing whether that was too much or too little. She got on the elevator, Rolf close at her side, and punched the button for the penthouse. On the way up, she rehearsed what she was going to say. She put a hand in her pocket and felt the roll of bills, her stake for the card game. Phil's emergency fund, provided by the

Department. They'd probably expect a receipt. The thought made her smile.

The elevator doors slid open. She stepped out and was immediately aware of two big, strong-looking goons who'd been standing against the wall. One of them stepped toward her and held out his hand, palm up.

Erin pretended not to understand. "I don't tip the muscle," she said and started to walk past him.

He sidestepped in front of her. "The gun, lady." His buddy started drifting around behind her.

"This is a registered police sidearm, smartass," she snapped, thinking, *everything is a test.* "I don't hand my piece over to anybody."

"And nobody gets in to talk to the boss with a gun," he retorted, squaring his shoulders to take up as much hallway space as possible.

"You've got a gun," she observed.

"That's different."

"Yeah. The difference is, the gun you're carrying is a Class B violent felony that'll get you five years, minimum. The gun I'm carrying is legit, and I'm responsible for it. Get out of my way."

For a second she thought he was going to make something happen, but he shuffled aside, muttering. She walked past him, Rolf eyeballing him and letting him know he'd better not try anything. They approached the door to Evan's suite. It appeared to be solid hardwood, with a brass knocker. Erin knocked.

The door opened. Yet another tough-looking guy met her. But he actually smiled in what appeared to be genuine friendliness.

"Erin O'Reilly? Good to meet you. Paddy Ryan, everyone calls me PR. C'mon in. This dog yours? He looks like one fine piece of work. How much a dog like that run you?"

"Seven or eight thousand," she said. "The Department paid for him."

Ryan whistled. "Wow. You oughta get him a gold-plated collar or something. The boss is in the den with the others. Everyone else got here already, but forget about it, you're not late or nothing. They're just shooting the shit and having drinks. Can I take your coat?"

"Sure." Amused by the talkative gangster, she handed over her jacket. He noticed the gun at her side but didn't mention it.

Evan's apartment was tastefully furnished with deep-pile carpet and heavy wood furniture. She passed through the dining room and saw what appeared to be a crystal chandelier hanging from the ceiling. Crime had definitely paid where Evan O'Malley was concerned.

The den was paneled in dark wood with dark green carpet. The O'Malley leadership were seated around the card table in the center. Erin knew all the faces. There was Evan, cold-eyed and careful. At his right hand was Mickey Connor, overflowing his chair, a glass of whiskey in his hand and no expression at all on his face. Next to him was Veronica Blackburn, the woman in charge of the O'Malley sex trade, a face starting to show the lines of middle age perched atop an impossibly youthful and well-endowed body. She doubtless employed a high-priced plastic surgeon. Keeping an empty seat between Veronica and himself was Corky Corcoran, in the middle of a humorous story about a pair of drunken Irish priests. At Corky's elbow, disheveled and staring into space, sat Kyle Finnegan. Finnegan worked with union rackets and handled other personnel matters for the O'Malleys. He was widely believed to be utterly insane. Finally, on Finnegan's right, Maggie Callahan completed the circle. Maggie was small, mousy, quiet, and didn't look like any criminal Erin had ever seen. She was the dealer in the group's card games. Erin had never been quite clear what

Maggie did for the O'Malleys. She had no record and hardly ever spoke or made eye contact with anyone else.

Evan politely stood. Corky bounced to his feet and, after a moment, the others followed suit.

"Miss O'Reilly, welcome," Evan said. "Thank you for taking time out of your busy schedule to join us. Before you sit down, I'm afraid there's a simple preliminary precaution. Please don't be offended."

The look in his eyes made it clear he didn't care if she was offended or not. Mickey lumbered toward her.

"Okay, O'Reilly, hands out to either side," he growled, reaching toward her.

Everything's a test, Erin thought again. "The hell I will," she snapped, taking a step back from Mickey and dropping a hand close to, but not quite on, the butt of her Glock. "That gorilla's hands don't touch me."

"We gotta make sure you're clean," Mickey said, not backing down.

"You think I'm wearing a goddamn wire?" Erin exploded. She let her voice carry the full weight of her Long Island upbringing. "Oh yeah, you'd like that, wouldn't you? Any excuse to feel up a woman. That may be how you get your kicks, but it takes more than that to get me going. Look, Mr. O'Malley, no disrespect, but your boy here is being kind of rude, and he's making me feel unwelcome. You think I'm recording you? You invited me here! I'm here because you want me to be. But I get it, if you don't want that, I can go home. Forget about it, no problem."

Mickey glanced at Evan, whose expression didn't change.

"Miss O'Reilly, it's not my intention to make you uncomfortable," Evan said. "I suggest a compromise. Miss Blackburn will ensure all's as it ought to be. If you'll kindly step down the hall to the spare bedroom, you'll have the necessary privacy."

Erin hadn't expected the mob boss to be so accommodating. She couldn't very well refuse what was, in fact, a reasonable request. "Sure, if that's how you want to play it," she said. "But she's not going to find any wire on me."

"We'll see about that, honey," Veronica said. She took Erin's arm just above the elbow and walked with her out of the room on six-inch heels, hips swinging. Rolf trotted beside Erin.

Veronica closed the bedroom door behind them and flicked on the light. "All right, honey, now it's just us girls," she said with a bright, white-toothed smile. "So tell me. How's Cars?"

"He'll be fine," Erin said.

Veronica looked confused. Then she smiled again, more widely than before. "Oh, you thought I meant... no, I mean, how is he?" She cocked her head toward the bed. "I've never had him, and I'm just dying to know."

Erin opened her mouth. Then she closed it again. "You have no idea," she finally said. Rolf, beside her, cocked his head curiously at Veronica.

"No, I'm afraid I don't," Veronica said. As she spoke, she stepped in close. Erin caught a heavy, sensuous scent wafting off the other woman. To her surprise, she recognized it. It was Heartbreaker fragrance, which put her in mind of a very unpleasant previous case.

"You hear things about men, of course," Veronica went on, frisking Erin as she spoke. Her hands were less businesslike and more interested than Erin wanted. Rolf's hackles rose slightly. He was aware something was a little bit off, but Erin didn't give him any instructions, and there didn't seem to be a fight going on, so the K-9 stayed put.

"They all have reputations," Veronica said. "But get them between the sheets and sometimes you find out it's just talk. Take Corky, for example."

"Never had the pleasure," Erin tossed back at her.

"Of course not, honey," Veronica said, clearly not believing a word of it. "You don't mind if I check your underwire, do you? Sometimes people hide things there. I've never understood it. After all, most of the people who'd be checking you over are men, and the last thing you want to do is give them an excuse to touch you... here. Hmm, not bad. All natural. That's a fine money-making bod you've got there, honey."

"Thanks," Erin said dryly. She supposed it had been meant as a compliment.

"Now, Corky, talk to anybody and they'll tell you what a fantastic lover he is," Veronica said. "But it's all smoke and mirrors, honey. All bluff and bluster. I've had better than him plenty of times. I've been meaning to try him out again, though. Maybe he just had an off day. Even the Yankees strike out sometimes."

"Yeah," Erin said. To her relief, the other woman stopped touching her and stepped back.

"You're clean," Veronica said, in tones of slight disapproval. "And I do think we could do something more with your lingerie."

"I wasn't planning on showing it to anybody this evening," Erin said.

"You should always be prepared, honey. Sexiness is a state of mind more than body. You always know what you've got on underneath. And when opportunity comes knocking, you want him to fall on his ass when you open the door."

"And who's your opportunity this evening?" Erin asked.

"Who else? The big man at the table."

"Evan?" Erin blurted out. It didn't surprise her that Veronica would want to take him to bed. It surprised her that the madam thought she had a chance of succeeding.

"No, not Evan," Veronica said dismissively. "He's so old-school and strait-laced, he probably does it with the lights off. If he was ice cream, he'd be straight vanilla. And he's exactly the wrong kind of married. No, I mean the *big* man."

"Mickey," Erin said in a flat, expressionless voice.

"Have you seen him with his shirt off?" Veronica asked, licking her lips. "He's not quite in fighting trim anymore, but the muscles on him... my God."

"You'll have to tell me how it works out," Erin said, feeling a sudden urge to change the subject to almost anything else. "Why don't we get back to the table? The others will be wanting to start the game."

"Which game, honey?" Veronica purred. "I can think of about five going on right now between these participants, and that's just the ones I know about. I hope you know how to handle yourself, or someone else will end up doing it for you."

"I'll take my chances," Erin said, and with that she managed to get to the bedroom door and open it. She and Rolf walked quickly back to the den, trailed by Veronica. The madam had trouble moving fast in her ridiculous heels.

"Clean as a whistle," Veronica announced to the room.

"And I'm certain you checked as thoroughly as she'd permit you," Corky said. He motioned to the chair next to him. "If you'd care to sit, Erin, love?"

"Corcoran to the right, Blackburn to the left," Finnegan said to Erin. "Scylla and Charybdis. What's poor Odysseus to do?"

"Um... what?" Erin asked.

"Odysseus," Finnegan repeated. "Also called Ulysses, as in the work of the same name by James Joyce, greatest writer of

Ireland, who also wrote *Finnegan's Wake*, which isn't about me. As far as I know."

"Right," Erin said. She had no idea what he was talking about. To judge from the reactions around the table, neither did anyone else.

"It could be about you, lad," Corky said. "It's not like anyone has the least bloody idea what Joyce is talking about in any of his books. I tried to read one once. Next thing I knew, I was in a pub in Galway, it was two days later, I'd the mother of all hangovers, and I was wearing another man's shirt."

"Sounds like an odyssey," Finnegan observed. "Maybe you were the first man in Ireland to really read Joyce the proper way."

"We gonna play cards or what?" Mickey asked.

"A splendid idea, Mr. Connor," Evan said. "Maggie, if you'd care to do the honors? Mr. Ryan will take orders for refreshments. I'll have a whiskey sour."

"Scotch," Mickey said. "Straight."

"I'll have an Irish special, in honor of my absent mate," Corky said. "You ken what I mean?"

"Car bomb?" Ryan guessed.

"And they call you PR," Corky said. "Don't you know it's poor public relations calling it that? And to say it to an Irishman's face? I'm thinking I need to teach you some manners."

"Hey, sorry," Ryan said, taking a step back and putting up his hands. "I didn't mean nothing by it."

"Nay, lad, I'm just taking the piss," Corky laughed. "That'll be grand."

"I'll have a Schlitz beer," Finnegan said. "In honor of Detroit."

"Lad, Schlitz comes from Milwaukee," Corky said. "That's not even the same bloody state. I don't know Detroit, but I know beer."

"I drank a Schlitz in Detroit," Finnegan said. "In the company of three men I thought were my friends. All of them dead, now."

"Hopefully not from drinking the beer," Corky added.

"I'll have Glen D whiskey, if you've got it," Erin said.

"We get it straight from the source," Ryan said. "Fresh off the boat."

"I'll have a high stakes, honey," Veronica said.

"A which?" Ryan asked. He clearly wasn't a bartender.

"It's a cocktail," she said. "An ounce each of vodka, mango rum, cherry brandy, orange juice, and pineapple juice. It's best if the juice is fresh, but I don't know that Mr. O'Malley has any fresh pineapple, so I'll take it out of a can if I have to. Add a tablespoon of Jägermeister and strain it into ice. And make sure the Jägermeister is the herbal liqueur."

"Herbal liqueur?" Ryan repeated with a helpless look at his employer.

"Just do the best you can, Mr. Ryan," Evan said. "And Maggie will have a mineral water."

As Ryan retreated to the kitchen, mumbling Veronica's order under his breath in a hopeless attempt to remember it correctly, Maggie shuffled the cards.

"Antes, ladies and gentlemen," Evan said.

"Ooh, let's play," Veronica said, and Erin started at the feel of the other woman's foot against her calf.

Everything's a test, Erin thought for the third time that night. "Yeah, let's," she said as coolly as she could, sliding her leg out of contact. "I could use some extra pocket change."

Chapter 14

Erin wasn't a very good card player. She knew the rules, she was good at reading people, but when it came to the careful calculation of the odds, she was glad she was playing with someone else's money. As her stack of chips gradually shrank, she was also glad the point of the evening wasn't to play Texas hold 'em. The point was for Evan O'Malley to take the pulse of his organization and make sure everything was under control.

For Erin, of course, the point was to get in with the O'Malleys. But she knew not to be too forward or talkative. Better to let the others lead and see where the talk led. So she sipped her whiskey slowly, not wanting to get impaired, and listened.

Veronica and Corky carried most of the conversation at first. Though they were careful to talk around illegal activities, Erin gathered that Corky's transportation business was going as well as usual. He was also eager to talk about Mexico.

"It's a grand country," he said. "All sorts of untapped potential. I'm thinking, if we're ever needing a change of scenery, the coyote business has promise."

"I've heard coyotes are decent eating if they haven't sat too long on the highway," Finnegan remarked.

"Bringing folk across the border," Corky explained. "The lads who do that are called coyotes. The difficulty would be brokering some manner of agreement with the lads currently running it."

"Those lads are a bit touchy," Evan said. Erin knew he was talking about Mexican drug cartels. Touchy was an understatement.

"All the same, as long as we steered clear of the high-end merchandise, I'm thinking there's an opening," Corky said. "And it could be a channel for importing all manner of other things." Erin guessed high-end merchandise was his euphemism for drugs.

"That reminds me," Erin said. "Liam McIntyre was at the last one of these games I sat in on."

"God rest his soul," Corky said.

"Will someone else be taking his place soon? In the game?"

"You're looking at her," Veronica said smugly.

Erin filed that information away for further consideration. It meant Veronica, in addition to handling prostitution for the O'Malleys, had been promoted to take over their drug business. That made her a very powerful woman in the organization, particularly if she'd set her sights on an alliance with Mickey.

"Congratulations," Erin said. "It's always good to see a working girl make good."

"Thanks, honey," Veronica purred.

"How about Cars?" Mickey said. "How long till he's back on his feet? If he ever is?"

"The doctors say he'll be fine," Erin said. "But he'll need some rest. I'm looking after him." By this she meant to suggest she was caring for his business interests as well as his physical well-being. Her implication hit home with everyone at the table, with the possible exceptions of Maggie and Finnegan, who didn't seem to be paying attention.

"It's quite a responsibility you've taken on," Evan said, looking her in the eye. "Particularly in these troubled times. Mr. Carlyle's staff are two men down at present. Are you looking into correcting this?"

"He needs a new head of security," Erin said. "We thought we should run the name by you first."

"I'm listening," Evan said.

"Ian Thompson."

The dead silence that followed was broken by a derisive snort from Mickey.

"I don't think that boy's gonna be guarding much except his own ass," he said. "Thin little guy like that better watch himself. He better not drop the soap in the shower at Riker's."

"He'll be out soon," Erin said coolly, turning her attention on Mickey. This was the big moment and she'd better get it right. "It took a little while to sort everything out, but I squared it. He should be on the street sometime tomorrow, free and clear."

"How do you figure?" Mickey asked. "Word is, he's been charged. Murder One. He'll be older than Cars before he gets out."

"The DA's having a change of heart," Erin said.

"How'd you swing it?" he demanded.

"It wasn't easy. Especially once we had the gun. It was a little careless to leave it so close to the site, but I'm sure that won't happen again. I wasn't able to do anything about the serial number. My people know the Beretta belongs to Ian and they've matched the ballistics. But I was able to muddy things enough that the DA couldn't make an airtight case. He likes his conviction rate and he's up for re-election soon. Plus, it's the second time we've arrested Ian recently and the optics aren't good. War hero, you know? It looks like harassment. With all that, I was able to make it happen."

"Well done," Evan said. "But what happens to the investigation?"

Erin shrugged. "We keep looking, but it's a gangland hit. Those aren't exactly a top priority for my squad. It'll sit on our desks for a week or two, until the next hot case comes down. Then I'll make sure it gets pushed to the back of the line."

Evan nodded. "And Mr. Thompson will be beholden to you for your courtesy."

"He'll be solid," Erin said. "He's a stand-up guy. He didn't say anything about anyone. And now we know he'll do what needs doing. He's a man who knows how to follow orders."

Mickey was staring at Erin. His jaw worked slowly, the muscles clenching. Erin wondered how quickly she could get her gun out, if she'd have time to get a shot off if he decided to jump over the table and murder her with his bare hands. But Carlyle's assessment had been accurate. Erin was taking credit for the hit on Caleb, and for getting her personal hitman off the hook, right in front of him, and he couldn't say a word about it. And Erin was angling to get Carlyle's security put under the care of the one man she knew to be personally loyal to him. A man who'd also saved her own life. Twice.

Evan nodded. "Once the lad's out, I'll have someone speak to him," he said. "We'll make certain he understands his new role. Now, I believe it's my bet. I'll lay fifty."

With that, they returned to the card game. Erin was feeling pretty good about the whole thing until her pair of fives lost the hand to Corky's two pair, eights over fives.

"Sorry, love," he said with a lopsided smile. "But a lad's got to take what he can in this world."

"Speaking of which," Finnegan said, "I have a question."

All heads turned toward him. Finnegan ran a hand through his uncombed, helter-skelter hair. He took a sip of his beer and examined his fingernails. Erin saw they were ragged, suggesting he was a nail-biter.

"Well, lad?" Corky finally asked.

"Oh. Right." Finnegan cleared his throat. "What's the purpose of a police force?"

"Target practice," Mickey muttered.

"Mr. Connor," Evan said quietly. "Police are off limits. You know the rules."

"He was making a joke," Veronica said. But Erin didn't think Mickey had much of a sense of humor.

"Friendly competition," Corky suggested, with a wink at Erin. "They keep the game interesting. If nobody's chasing you, how can you tell when you're supposed to run?"

"I think they're like lions," Veronica said.

"Really?" Erin asked, surprised. "How so?"

"They snap up the ones who can't keep up," Veronica said. "Once you get too slow, or too old, or just too careless, chomp! They eat you right up." She licked her lips. "They make sure we're all healthy and keep things from getting too crowded on the street. Weeding out the sick and the weak."

"And we uphold the law," Erin said, needled into saying something she immediately wished she hadn't.

Veronica and Corky both laughed. Erin didn't join in, but she managed a smile.

"Now that's how you tell a joke," Corky said to Mickey. Then he turned back to Erin. "Come, love, at least pretend to be serious. We all know no one becomes a copper just to keep people from breaking the law. That's like saying a lad chooses the Life because he wants to break laws. That's bloody nonsense. Lads in the Life are practical. So are coppers. How long have you been walking the beat?"

"Twelve years," she said.

"And you can't be such an idealist," he scoffed. "Not when you're sitting here with us tonight."

Erin let herself give a self-conscious smile, silently thanking Corky for throwing her a lifeline. "Nothing's black and white," she said. "Everyone has their own gray areas. I guess cops are mostly meant to keep civilians as safe as possible. You and me, we're in the game, but they're not. That's why no one really cares Caleb got clipped, but if some soccer mom goes down in Tribeca, it's all over the news."

"Miss O'Reilly's close to the truth," Finnegan said. "And Corky is, too. But you're all wrong."

"Enlighten us, Professor," Corky said. "Help us see the error of our ways."

"Police don't protect anyone," Finnegan said. "Particularly a unit like Miss O'Reilly's. Nineteen times out of twenty, they're just mopping up the blood after it's all gone down. And most killers, they don't kill again, so what's the point of locking them up?"

"Payback," Mickey said.

"Punishment," Veronica purred, leaning in and putting a hand on Mickey's enormous bicep.

"Wrong again," Finnegan said. "It's all part of the scam."

"What scam?" Erin asked.

"The illusion of security," he said. "The point of cops on every street corner isn't to make you safe, it's to make you *feel* safe. As long as the perception of safety is there, people don't care who dies. We could be living in the city with the worst murder rate in the world and it wouldn't matter, not as long as there's a cop within shouting distance. You know what kills most Americans?"

"Heart attacks and cancer," Erin said.

"Precisely," Finnegan said, pointing his finger at her like a gun barrel. "But does that stop us eating steaks and getting suntans? No, because we've decided we feel safe from those things, even though those are exactly the things that are killing us. How many New Yorkers get murdered in a year, Detective?"

"Three or four hundred," Erin said.

"Out of a city of eight million," Finnegan said. "And there's over thirty thousand police. Suppose half those coppers turned in their guns and went home. Would the murder rate double?"

There was silence around the table.

"I doubt it," Finnegan said after a moment. "But people might *feel* less safe. And that's unforgivable. So that is the purpose of a police force. It's all illusion, just like airport security. And Miss O'Reilly knows this quite well, or she wouldn't be sitting here with us." He paused and crinkled his brow in apparent confusion. "Does anyone else taste that?"

"You're the only one drinking Schlitz," Corky said.

"No," Finnegan said. "I taste... key lime pie. And anchovies. Nobody else?"

There was another silence, more awkward.

"Lad," Corky said, "you've convinced me. I'm never drinking that bloody beer."

Amid laughter, Maggie dealt the next hand.

* * *

Erin lost Phil's emergency undercover money. She would've liked to think it was bad luck, but in truth, she wasn't paying enough attention to the cards. Corky and Finnegan were the big winners. Evan, as he had the last time she'd seen him play, somehow managed to break almost exactly even. By the time he called the game, just before midnight, he'd made a net total of fifty dollars. Erin was flat broke, Veronica was hanging onto a hundred and fifty, Corky had more than doubled his stake, and Finnegan, apparently by accident, had a big stack of chips in front of him. He'd gone all in, Mickey had assumed he was bluffing, and had laid down a full house, the best hand of the night.

"Can't read a guy when his brain's scrambled," Mickey grumbled as Finnegan raked in the pot and left him almost wiped out.

"I was lucky," Finnegan said. "But we're all fortune's fools. The joker in a deck of cards used to be called the fool, I think. Which is also a tarot card. I wonder if you can tell fortunes with a normal deck of cards. If so, would the queen of spades be Death? Or the Lovers? Or maybe both?"

"I think that's enough for one night," Evan said, pushing his chair back from the table. He stood up. "Thank you for coming. As always, it's a pleasure."

The various O'Malleys got to their feet, finishing the last of their drinks. Paddy Ryan brought coats for those who'd worn them, handing a faux-fur wrap to Veronica and returning Erin's leather jacket. Finnegan started to leave, realized he was walking into a bedroom instead of the hallway, and returned muttering to himself.

"You okay to get home?" Erin asked him.

"I always find my way," he said. "Sometimes I go the long way round. Good talking to you, Miss O'Reilly. I like you. You remind me of someone I think I met once. But maybe not. It's hard to remember sometimes. But you're someone to watch. Tick-tock." He left while Erin was still trying to figure out what she was supposed to say in answer to that.

"Is he really as crazy as he acts?" she asked Corky in an undertone.

"Oh, he's precisely as mad as that," Corky said cheerfully. "But that doesn't mean it's not useful to him. It's a grand thing in the Life, being known to be crazy. Makes the other lads nervous."

"A moment, Miss O'Reilly, if you please?" Evan said.

"I'll be waiting outside," Corky said. "To walk you down to your car."

"Aren't you the gentleman tonight," she said.

"Don't be so sure," Veronica said. She whispered something into Mickey's ear, having to stretch to do it in spite of her high heels. Then she, Corky, and Mickey went out the door, followed by Maggie, who didn't say a word to anyone. Paddy made himself scarce, so it was just Erin and Evan standing next to the card table.

"I think I've underestimated you, Miss O'Reilly," Evan said softly.

Erin's stomach lurched. She tried to keep her face neutral while telling herself that if he was really suspicious of her, he'd have kept Mickey in the room with him.

"How so?" she asked, pleasantly surprised at how calm and level her voice sounded.

"I didn't think you were likely to act with such... initiative."

"I do what I have to," she said. "I take care of my business."

He nodded. "Do ask Mr. Thompson to be more careful in the future. He's had something of a narrow shave, I think."

"Forget about it," she said. "He understands the situation. It won't be a problem."

"I'm pleased to hear it. And do give my regards to Mr. Carlyle, when next you see him. Tell him he's missed."

"I'll do that," Erin said.

Evan offered his hand. Erin took it with a firm grip, looking him in the eye. His icy blue stare bored into her. She forced herself not to blink, even made herself smile slightly, a cocky, self-confident smile that was a hundred miles from how she was feeling.

He seemed to like what he saw, or at least to be satisfied with it. He let go of her hand. "I look forward to our further acquaintance," he said. "Enjoy the remainder of your evening."

*   *   *

"Where to now, love?" Corky asked as Erin stepped into the hallway. "The night's young, but we're getting no younger."

"I'm going to get some sleep," she said.

"Sleep? During the night? You're mad, love. That's not what the hours of darkness were made for."

Erin shook her head and smiled wearily. "I don't know how you do it. You're going to have a heart attack one of these days and just keel over dead."

"Aye, that's as may be, but they'll find me with a smile on my face," he said cheerfully.

The guards at the end of the hall politely stood to one side. Rolf stuck close to Erin while they waited for the elevator. The K-9 graciously permitted Corky to scratch his head.

When the doors opened, they got in and Corky pushed the button for the lobby. Erin glanced around the elevator car, looking for security cameras. She didn't see any, but she also didn't want to tempt fate, so she didn't say anything about their situation.

"Have you ever made it in an elevator, love?" Corky asked.

"What? No!"

"Ever been tempted?"

"Not really," she said. "There's no comfortable furniture, and I think you'd have to be pretty quick, unless you were riding all the way to the top of the Empire State Building."

"It has its ups and downs," he agreed pleasantly. "But it's a ride worth taking."

"Corky, is there any place you haven't had sex?"

That shut him up for most of the ride down. Just as the bell chimed for the lobby, he snapped his fingers triumphantly.

"A submarine," he said.

"Have you ever even been on a submarine?" she asked.

"I've not had the chance. That's probably why. Where are you parked?"

"Out and to the right, about half a block."

"Grand. I'll just see you make it to your car. I'd never forgive myself if something happened to you on my watch."

Erin looked at him. "How uncharacteristically chivalrous of you, Corky. But I'm fine."

He grinned. "I've no notion what you're saying, love. I'm the very soul of chivalry." He nodded pleasantly to the doorman on their way out into the night. Erin led the way to her Charger.

"Here we are," she said. "Goodnight."

"What, no kiss?" he asked, winking.

"Goodnight, Corky. And thank you."

"Don't mention it, love. I'll be seeing you."

Corky disappeared around the corner, hands in his pockets, whistling a cheery tune. Erin watched him go, shaking her head and smiling to herself. A moment later, she recognized the throaty rumble of his BMW convertible. Then she reached into her pocket for her car keys. She opened the back for Rolf, who hopped into his compartment. She closed him in and reached for the driver's door.

"Hold it."

The voice came from behind her. It was accompanied by a sudden growl from Rolf inside the car. Erin spun and dropped her keys, reaching reflexively for her Glock.

Mickey was quicker. His massive hand shot out, clamping down on Erin's arm. His fingers easily encircled her wrist with a grip so strong it might as well have been made of steel. He twisted her arm up and away from her belt as he stepped in close, pinning her against her car door.

Erin smelled his aftershave and the heavy, menacing scent of his body. She caught a whiff of Scotch on his breath and had to fight back her gag reflex. Where the hell had he come from? Why hadn't Rolf warned her? The dog was barking frantically inside the car, the sound muffled but ferocious.

"Let go of me," she demanded.

Mickey didn't budge. "What's your game, bitch?" he asked. He squeezed slightly. Pain shot up Erin's arm and she knew he could snap the bones like sticks. "What do you want?"

"Same thing everybody does," she retorted, trying to pull free. She had absolutely no chance of breaking that iron grip. Her mind raced. Mickey probably didn't mean to kill her, she told herself. But he'd dared lay hands on a police officer. All bets were off. She couldn't get at her sidearm, nor her backup piece at her ankle. She couldn't take him hand to hand. Now that it was too late, she fully appreciated what Carlyle had warned her about. At close quarters, Mickey Connor was terrifying.

"I'm supposed to believe you're doin' all this for love?" he demanded. "Of Cars?"

"You believe what you want to believe," she said.

"You got Evan convinced," he said, bending in even closer. Their eyes were only a few inches apart. "But I know some shit he don't. I know you and Thompson didn't pop Caleb. You don't have it in you. You want him to think you're one of us, but you're not. I got your number, bitch."

"If you've got it all figured out, then what are you asking me for?" Erin was playing for time. If she gave the wrong answer, she was now convinced Mickey would kill her. He was looking for an excuse. She had to save herself. She moved one of her feet slightly and felt it tap against her key fob on the sidewalk. A hint of an idea had come into her head. Rolf, only a few inches from her, was hurling himself at the glass, snarling and barking. He, at least, thought he could take Mickey up close.

"There's one thing I can't figure," Mickey said. "Who's calling the shots? You or that smooth son of a bitch Carlyle? Is this one of his plans? Or one of yours? He planning to take over from O'Malley? Or is this all some goddamn sting? Are you working for him, or for the cops? Well? Which is it?" He squeezed tighter, making Erin's eyes water.

The truth wouldn't save her. Neither would any lie she could think of. Erin set her foot on top of her car keys, feeling with the toe of her shoe. "Fuck you, Connor," she spat.

He smiled then. "You got a mouth on you, girl," he said. "I wonder how far down your throat I could ram my fist, right between those pretty lips. I'm thinking all the way to my elbow. Turn you inside out. You got anything smart to say to that?"

Erin pressed down with her foot. Her toe was squarely on the panic button. The Charger's lights flashed and the piercing tone of her car alarm shredded the air. Mickey flinched in surprise and his hold loosened just for a second. Erin dropped a hand to her belt. She had no space to draw her gun, but she wasn't aiming for the gun.

"Yeah," Erin said. "*Fass!*"

As she spoke, she hit the release button for Rolf's compartment. The window popped open right next to her head. Rolf, a ninety-pound furry missile, shot out of the car. His jaws snapped shut on Mickey's arm. The mobster let go of Erin and stumbled back a step.

Any normal man would have been dragged to the ground by the weight of the German Shepherd. Mickey bared his own teeth, grabbed Rolf's jaw with his free hand, and wrenched it open, tossing the dog aside. It was an unbelievable display of raw strength. Erin had never seen anyone manage it before.

Neither had Rolf. The K-9 tumbled through the air with a startled yelp and landed heavily on his side.

Erin ducked, dove, and rolled across the sidewalk, trying to put space between her and Mickey. She clawed at her belt, found the grip of her Glock, and yanked it out of its holster. She came up on one knee, pointing the gun at Mickey.

He stood there, chest heaving, blood running down his arm, staring at her. And he was still smiling.

"What you gonna do with that?" he asked. "You gonna shoot me? I'm not attacking you. I'm not armed. Your dog bit me. Call him off."

Rolf was back on his feet, growling, tensed to spring back into action. He didn't seem to be badly hurt.

"*Bleib,*" Erin hissed at him. He bristled but obeyed, staying put.

Mickey's smile only widened, like a shark about to bite.

"I think IA's going to believe my side of the story," Erin said. Her finger was inside the guard, tight against the Glock's trigger. The Glock 19 had a 5.5-pound trigger pull and she knew she was putting at least three pounds on it already. She felt the tension in the poised firing pin. Just a little more and she'd send a nine-millimeter round into Mickey's chest.

"Funny thing," he said, seeming unconcerned. "Video phones. Everybody's got 'em now. Suppose there was someone, say, across the street, filming this? They get a clip of you shooting an unarmed man, ten feet away. What's that? That's murder."

Erin thought he was bluffing. But what if he wasn't? And then she thought, why did that matter? Was she really considering gunning this man down in cold blood? It wouldn't just prove to Evan she was a gangster. It would prove it to herself.

What she should do was take him in, haul his ass downtown, book him for aggravated assault on a police officer. But she couldn't do that, either. Not without compromising the operation. Because what would Evan do if she arrested his chief enforcer?

"See, that's your problem," Mickey said, as if reading her thoughts. "You still got rules. I don't."

"You touch my dog again, I'll blow your goddamn brains out," she promised. "Rules or no rules."

"Your dog bites me again, I'll feed him his own teeth," Mickey retorted. "Same for you, bitch. I know you."

"I don't think so," Erin said. "If you did, you'd know to stay the hell away from me. You think you're tough? I'm the toughest bitch in the toughest gang in this city. Don't forget it. And don't push me."

"I don't forget nothing," Mickey said. "And if you fuck with me, or with Evan, you're gonna find out how much damage I can do. I'll make you hurt in ways you don't even know about." Then, as if they hadn't just had a near-death encounter, as if they hadn't threatened to kill one another, he casually turned his back on her and walked away.

The worst moment, in a way, was right then. Erin still had her Glock aimed at Mickey. She very nearly pulled the trigger. One shot, into the back of his head, and a huge problem would be solved.

"God," she whispered. Was she really that close to becoming what she pretended to be?

"Let him go, kiddo," she said quietly to Rolf. "We'll get him. I promise. Just not tonight."

But the Shepherd's hackles stayed up all the way back to Sean and Michelle's house.

Chapter 15

She didn't dare call Phil from the car. She parked, got Rolf out of his compartment, and walked into the park across the street from her brother's house. At this late hour it was deserted; she saw no one, not even a neighbor out for a late-night stroll. She took out Phil's phone and called him.

He picked up on the first ring, wide awake and anxious. "Hello?"

"Hey, Phil, it's me."

"How'd it go?"

"Great. Well, except for the part at the end where Mickey Connor tried to kill me."

"He did what?!" Phil had sounded alert before. Now he sounded alarmed.

"Relax, Phil. It's fine. I slipped him."

"No, that's not fine, Erin. You have to come in. Terminate the assignment."

"I can't do that."

"Of course you can! Erin, when one of our officers is in danger, we don't leave them hanging. This is your life we're talking about."

"Yeah, Phil. My life. *Mine.* Listen, Mickey went for me because he doesn't trust me. I already knew that. But he didn't know what I was up to. The cover story hasn't been broken. He thinks I'm with Carlyle, trying to take over the O'Malleys."

"You're saying that like it's a good thing. It's not. If he assumes you're a gangster, he'll treat you like one. You've seen *The Godfather*. You know what happens to the crooked police captain."

"I'll just have to avoid Italian restaurants. Which is too bad. I like Italian food."

He sighed. "Erin, this isn't a joke and it's not funny."

"I know. But you've got to trust me, Phil. I know what I'm doing."

"No one's ever done this before. There's no script, no playbook. *Nobody* knows what you're doing, least of all you."

"Then why second-guess me?"

"I've never had one of my officers get killed undercover. I don't want you to be the first."

Erin smiled. "I'd hate to ruin your perfect record. But I've got a pretty good record of not getting killed myself."

He chuckled and let the subject drop. "So, Evan O'Malley bought your version of events? What'd you tell him?"

"I implied I was behind the hit on Caleb Carnahan."

Erin could've sworn she felt suction through the phone from Phil's intake of breath.

"You told him that?" Phil asked. She marveled at his mild, level tone of voice.

"Implied it," she repeated. "I let him believe I had Ian shoot Caleb."

He whistled. "But Ian didn't do it?"

"No. Mickey Connor killed Caleb."

"You have proof of that?"

"No. But either he pulled the trigger or he had one of his guys do it. I'd bet my pension on it."

"You might be betting more than that. No wonder he's mad at you. Did Evan order the hit?"

"No."

"You're sure?"

"I wasn't sure at the start. But I am now. Evan's been trying to figure out how Siobhan Finneran got close to Carlyle and me. He knows someone set us up, someone inside. It had to be either Ian or Caleb. So he took both of them in for questioning. But he left them for a few hours after interviewing them. If he'd been sure, he'd have taken care of the perp right away. I think Evan told Mickey to let both of them go, but to keep an eye on them. Ian walked, but a couple of goons took Caleb away."

"Why'd he let Ian go? Why not kill both of them?"

"Mickey needed a fall guy. An unsolved murder is fine, but it's even better if you get one of your enemies to take the hit for you. While Mickey had his guys watching Ian and Caleb, he went to Ian's apartment. He got the key off the landlord, raked the lock on Ian's gun locker, and swiped one of his handguns. Then he made sure Ian got released in time to go home, get his gun, and go out and shoot Caleb. In the meantime, he worked Caleb over."

"What for?"

"That was a mistake," she said. "Mickey's smarter than he looks, but he runs on impulse. When he's got a guy he's going to kill, he just can't keep his hands off the poor schmuck. He can't help himself. He's got to be in on it, up close and personal. He could've shot me tonight, but he just had to use his hands. That's probably the reason I'm still breathing.

"He beat the crap out of Caleb," she continued, "then took him behind the Barley Corner, shot him in the face, and ditched the gun where he knew we'd find it. We'd trace the gun back to Ian and that'd be the end of the case. It almost worked, too."

"But why did he kill Caleb in the first place, if Evan didn't want him to?" Phil asked.

Erin had been thinking about this. "Because Mickey's the one who used Caleb to set us up. He tried to maneuver Siobhan to kill Carlyle and me."

"That's a lot of trouble to go to," Phil said. "I've seen Mickey's file. He doesn't hesitate to get his hands dirty and he's perfectly capable of killing Carlyle himself."

"You're right about that," Erin said, suppressing a shudder as she remembered Mickey's strength and speed. "Mickey can't take out Carlyle without Evan's permission. That'd be suicide. But he wants Carlyle out of his way. There's a shakeup going on in the O'Malleys. Evan's still at the top, but he's losing his grip, and everybody else knows it. Evan thinks he's got Mickey's loyalty, but I think Mickey's getting ready to replace him. He's got Veronica Blackburn in his corner, and she just got promoted to handle their drug trade. Between her drugs and her girls, that's where they get a lot of their income, and Mickey controls most of their muscle. They've nearly got a lock on the organization."

"Who's on the other side?"

"Carlyle and Corky. Corky can handle himself in a fight, and Carlyle's no coward, but they're not muscle guys. Corky has his contacts through the Teamsters and some of the other unions, and Carlyle's got their gambling and money laundering. They're powerful, but they'll probably lose if it comes to a straight fight."

"What about the rest of the O'Malleys?" Phil asked. "Where do they line up?"

"I don't know. Kyle Finnegan's hard to figure. I expect he'll just wait and watch and join the winning side. Barring that, he'll side with whoever he likes most on any given day. That guy's something else, Phil. I think he's actually crazy. I mean, out of his mind. And that's about it for their senior leadership. The rest will follow their bosses, probably."

"So you think a full-on war is brewing?"

"I think it's already started. Siobhan was the first shot."

"And you're on the front lines. Erin, you've got guts to spare, but this is a really dangerous situation."

"I know. But I don't have much choice. I have to do this, Phil."

"Okay. I understand."

"You do?"

"Erin, when I was a rookie, pounding pavement, one day this young woman asked me to help her. Her dog had broken its leash and run off in Central Park. She was worried sick. The dog was having the time of its life, running all over the place, but it wouldn't come when called. I went to a hot dog cart and asked for a plain wiener, no bun. Then I got upwind of the mutt and let him get a good whiff. He came right up to me, I grabbed him by the collar, and brought him back. The woman was... well, she was pretty happy. Her name was Camilla. We got to talking, and we'll be married fifteen years as of next week."

"Congratulations."

"Thank you. If she was in trouble, I don't think there's a single thing I wouldn't do to save her. But I'd also try to make sure she didn't go doing anything reckless or dangerous on my behalf. Love's wonderful, Erin, but it can make us do some very foolish things."

"You don't have to tell me that," she said with a dry chuckle.

"So, let's consider the tactical situation," he said. "You've taken credit for a hit you didn't perform. Do you think Mickey will tell his boss the truth?"

"No. Because that would mean admitting he'd disobeyed an order from Evan."

"Then you don't have to worry about Evan himself, just Mickey and his people. Will he make another attempt on you?"

"I don't know. Probably. I better check under my car from now on. And I better move out of my brother's house. I don't want to put them in danger."

"That's a good idea. Make sure you go somewhere safe."

"I've got a safe place in mind."

"Good. Now, what's your next move?"

"Ian's getting released as we speak. Probably by morning. Evan thinks I arranged that, too. He'll provide protection for Carlyle."

"So Evan believes you've got sway with the DA's office. That's good, over the short term. Long-term, it'll cause problems."

"Like what?"

"What will you do if he asks you to take care of another problem for him?"

"You mean, let someone guilty out of jail? We might be able to rig something. I'd have to take that to the Captain."

"No, Erin," he said gently. "I mean, what will you do if he asks you to kill someone else?"

"Oh." Erin swallowed. "I guess maybe we better figure out how to get that wire on me without people finding it. If I can get a recording of Evan ordering it, we can put him away. I won't kill for him, obviously."

"That's right. Just remember, it will probably happen at some point, now that he thinks you're that kind of cop."

"Maybe I shouldn't have played it this way," she said.

"No, it was a good instinct, and the more criminal he thinks you are, the better, at this point."

"So the operation's still on?"

He sighed again. "Yes, for now, if that's what you want. Just be careful."

"Copy that. Goodnight, Phil."

"Goodnight, Erin."

She went into the O'Reilly brownstone as quietly as she could, but by the time she got her shoes off, Michelle was standing on the upstairs landing.

"Everything okay?" Michelle asked.

Erin had the sudden, mad impulse to say, *Yeah, Shelley, except for the part where an ex-prizefighter tried to ram his fist down my throat.* That would get her sister-in-law's attention.

"It went fine," she said instead. "Business as usual."

*   *   *

Erin slept like a rock, without any of the nightmares she expected. She woke up with a headache, but with some of her energy restored, ready to take care of business. The first thing she did was take Rolf for their morning jog. She made sure to carry a pistol with her, but they met no gangsters. After that, she took a shower and grabbed breakfast. She met Anna and Patrick on their way to school and had to pause to give and receive hugs. Michelle looked at her with concern, but didn't say anything and Erin didn't offer any information.

Then it was out to her car to check the New York State Department of Corrections database on her computer. As she'd told Phil she would, she did a quick sweep of the car with Rolf, looking for explosives. Finding no car bombs, she got in and pulled up Ian's information. According to the database, he was set to be released at eight-thirty, which was in an hour. Erin accordingly set off for Riker's Island. It was normally about a forty-five minute drive, but morning traffic made it longer. She used the lights and sirens a little, just to move things along.

She got to the prison almost on time, displayed her police credentials, and hurried to the indicated entrance. She left Rolf in the car, which didn't make him happy.

Ian was on his way out when she got there. Erin was glad to see he looked intact. She knew inmates didn't get shanked as often as they did in the movies, but she'd still been worried. The O'Malleys had enemies locked up at Riker's and they would've welcomed an opportunity to stick it to one of the Irishmen.

"Morning," she said.

"Good morning, ma'am," he said. If he was surprised to see her, he didn't show it.

"Thought you might need a ride downtown," she said.

"Not necessary," he said. "But thanks. I appreciate it."

As they walked to Erin's Charger, she glanced around to make sure no one was close enough to overhear. "You okay?" she asked.

"Yes, ma'am."

"Sorry about this whole thing."

"Not your fault. I should've secured my weapons better."

"Ian," she said. "I know who did this to you."

"So do I, ma'am."

"What are you planning on doing about it?" she asked.

"Not sure we should be having this conversation, ma'am," he said. His face was completely unreadable.

"That's what I thought. I'm asking, hell, I'm *ordering* you. Whatever you're planning on doing, don't."

"With all due respect, you're not my commanding officer, ma'am."

"I'm speaking for Carlyle on this. Don't go gunning for Mickey Connor. Stand down."

He stopped walking. Erin faced him. She couldn't believe this. Here they stood, on the pavement outside the most notorious prison in New York City, talking about committing murders.

"I don't understand, ma'am," he said.

"I'm a detective, Ian. If you go hunting for this son of a bitch, I'll have to bust you, and next time, the charges will stick. Vic's an asshole sometimes, but he's right. You can't just go around shooting people. You're not at war anymore."

"With respect, ma'am, that's where you're wrong. War is exactly what's going on here, and you know it."

Erin sighed. It was as if he'd been listening to her conversation with Phil. "You're right, damn it all. But that doesn't change things. Carlyle and I have plans that'll take Mickey out of the picture, without you needing to do anything."

"It's a political solution, then?" he asked. "Not military?"

"Yeah, if you want to think of it like that."

"Never liked politicians much, ma'am. Don't like to think of you being one."

She smiled. "I don't like them myself. But sometimes they're necessary. Look, if he comes after you head-on, I'm not saying you can't shoot back. But don't start anything, okay? You nearly went down for this murder. I can't protect you from everything."

"I'm not asking you to, ma'am. Don't need any top-cover."

"Have you got a death wish, Ian?"

He shrugged. "Don't really feel one way or the other about it."

"You got anything you still want to do before you check out?"

"Yes, ma'am."

"Then work with me on this. Carlyle and I need you. With Caleb gone, you'll be in charge of security at the Corner. I already squared it with Evan. I swear, this will be worth it in the end, but you've got to hang tough for a while. I know you can do that."

She saw the subtle straightening of his already-upright posture, the squaring of his shoulders. "Yes, ma'am."

"And thank you, Ian," she said. "For everything you've already done. For Carlyle and for me. I won't forget it."

"Just doing my job, ma'am."

"That's bullshit and you know it. Now, I'm heading back to Manhattan. You coming?"

"Affirmative, ma'am."

Chapter 16

Erin dropped Ian at his apartment. She offered to walk him in, just in case Mickey had people waiting, but Ian shook his head.

"I'll be fine, ma'am," he said. "You've done plenty for me."

On reflection, Erin felt pity for any O'Malley goon who thought he could take Ian Thompson, even unarmed.

She wanted to visit Carlyle, but she'd used up too much of her morning already. She hurried to Precinct 8, arriving around nine-thirty to find Vic leaning back in his chair and sipping an enormous Mountain Dew.

"Where's the Lieutenant?" Erin asked.

"Leadership seminar," Vic said in a flat deadpan. "Bunch of bureaucrats think they can make him a better officer by showing him PowerPoint presentations. Where you been?"

"I had a couple errands to run," she said.

"I see Thompson got sprung," Vic said. "You gonna tell me your suspect for the Carnahan hit?"

"I'd like to."

"But you're not going to?"

Erin shook her head. "We can't make it stick with what we've got."

"So tell me what you do have, and maybe we can find something more."

She looked at him unhappily. Vic took a long slurp of soda and looked back.

"I've been doing some thinking," he said.

"About what?"

"You."

"In your lonely dreams."

He didn't smile. "This whole thing's been a rotten mess from the beginning. But I've got it narrowed down to three possibilities. Either you're the dumbest cop in the world, or you're as dirty as a pedophile priest."

"That's only two choices," she said.

"I know you're not dumb," Vic went on, as if she hadn't said anything. "And whatever you are, you're not dirty. So that leaves option three."

"Am I supposed to guess?"

"You're running an undercover op," he said, not taking his eyes off her.

"Vic," she said slowly, "even if that was true, you know I wouldn't be allowed to talk about it."

"Yeah," he said. "You've been learning from Carlyle. He's real good at not answering questions. Problem is, a non-answer is still an answer, just like not doing anything is an action. Way I figure it, you didn't mean to get in so deep with Carlyle, and now the only way out is to bend over for Keane. How bad are you getting screwed?"

"I don't bend over for anybody," Erin retorted. "Least of all him."

"You put out for Internal Affairs or they take your shield," he guessed. "That about the shape of it?"

"I don't work for IA," she snapped. "Not now, not ever. And we need to stop talking about this. Keep your voice down!"

"Well, if it isn't IA," Vic said in a lower tone, "then you're working something for the Captain. And the only thing that makes sense is the O'Malleys."

"Shut up, Vic. I mean it."

He nodded. "Okay. That's what I thought. I'm still pissed, you know."

"Do you ever stop?"

A slight smile quirked a corner of his mouth. "Guess not. But you could've trusted me on this. I'd have had your back."

"So you're mad that I hypothetically didn't break protocol on an alleged undercover operation?"

The smile got larger. "Yeah. Because there's two thousand pages in the Patrol Guide, they're all full of rules, and you're breaking some of them right now. But you shouldn't break the ones that matter."

"Which ones are those?"

"Don't kill the wrong people, don't take dirty money, and don't lie to your partner."

"They should put that on a T-shirt," Erin said. "Or maybe a bumper sticker."

"Okay, tell you what," Vic said. "I'll say this, and then I won't bring it up again. If this is what's going on, if you're running your guy as an informant to take down Old Man O'Malley, then I'll help you out with it. Because I hate all those bastards. But don't ask me to fall in love with your Irish pretty boy, 'cause I won't. As far as I'm concerned, he's still one of them, and if he's helping you it's just to save his own skin."

"That's not—" Erin began.

"But that doesn't matter," Vic rode right over her objection. "Because you're not one of them. For a little while I thought maybe you were, but it was just one of those optical illusion things. You know, like when you think the stairs are going up but they're really going down. So I don't give a shit about him, but you're one of us, and I've got your back. That good enough for you?"

"I guess it'll have to be," she said.

"Good. Now, I assume your reluctance to open up about the current case is part of this thing we're not talking about anymore?"

Erin nodded.

"So we lay off it and it hurts our closure rate," he grumbled.

"Not forever," she said. "We'll get him, one of these days."

"I hate waiting," Vic said.

"Patience is a virtue," Erin reminded him.

"I hate virtue, too."

"You hate everything."

"Only before ten AM. After that I mellow out a little."

"Vic?"

"Yeah?"

"Thanks."

"For what?"

"For figuring it out. And for understanding."

He rolled his eyes. "God. We having an Oprah moment, here? Am I supposed to give you a hug?"

"You try it and I'll Tase you in the nuts."

He grinned. "At least you'll have a nice big target."

"Too much information, Vic."

"Too much in every way," he said, still grinning.

"You still want that free swing at me?"

"You offering?"

"Take your best shot." Erin put her hands on her hips and stood in front of him, presenting a target.

He considered her for a moment. "Nah," he said. "Too easy."

And Erin felt a little bit better, because they were back to okay. "So what are we doing?" she asked.

"Sounds like we're spinning wheels on the Carnahan job," Vic said. "But you know those gangland hits. Hardest cases to close. Could've been anybody, inside or outside the O'Malleys. And anyway, it's a public-service homicide. I don't think Carnahan's likely to be missed."

She smiled gratefully. "But we'll leave it open," she said. "Just in case any new information comes to light."

"You never know," he said, finishing his Mountain Dew. "Hey, how close do you think I can get this cup to that wastebasket over there?"

"With all that caffeine giving you the jitters? You won't even hit the rim. How can you drink that stuff, anyway? Just watching you do it, I feel like my risk of diabetes goes up."

"It's like everything in life," he said, launching the empty cup across the room. It bounced off the edge of the trash can, spun up into the air, and landed against the wall. "Do it long enough and you get used to it. Do it a little longer, you start to like it."

*　　*　　*

The day was refreshingly quiet. They spent it following up on leads from cold cases, filling out paperwork, and doing all the other everyday chores that made a detective's life less glamorous than people thought. Erin took Rolf out for a couple of hours of training in the midafternoon. The K-9 needed several hours a week to keep him sharp. Of course, he didn't think of it as training. He thought it was fun.

Webb came back from his leadership seminar grouchy. That was good, in that it didn't make his mood noticeably worse when Erin and Vic told him they didn't have any new leads on Caleb's murder.

"Keep your ear to the ground with the O'Malleys," he told Erin. "Maybe someone will let something slip."

"I'll do that, sir," Erin said. It was nice to be able to tell him a little of the truth, at least.

At the end of the day, she headed to Bellevue Hospital. The same nurse was on duty, so she had an easy time getting through to Carlyle's room. A uniformed officer was on guard, though his attention was mainly focused on a crossword puzzle.

"Hey, Detective," he said when she flashed her gold shield. "You guys are smart, right?"

"Sometimes."

"I got this clue, I can't figure it out. What's a seven-letter word for a devious trick, first two letters F-A, ending in O-N-E?"

Erin paused, her hand on the door. What would be devious by the standards of the New York Times? What would Carlyle say? "I think it's two words, not one," she said after a moment. "Haven't you ever seen anybody pull a fast one?"

"Fast one. Got it." He grinned. "Thanks. Maybe those fancy shields aren't just for looks, huh?"

She returned the smile and went in.

Carlyle lay there, propped slightly upright, watching the TV. When he saw her, his eyes lit up.

"Good evening, darling," he said. "I'd greet you properly, but this bullet in my belly's still playing merry hell with my etiquette."

"Don't sweat it," she said. "How are you feeling?"

"I'll mend. Your brother did a grand job, and you can tell him so from me. Turn off the telly and let me know what's happening."

"I think we'll leave it on," she said.

"Background noise, in case anyone's listening? Erin, you're a natural at this business."

"That's sweet of you to say." She kissed him lightly, carefully. "Ian's out of Riker's."

"You're certain?"

"Yeah, I gave him a ride myself."

"Grand."

"I also ordered him not to shoot Mickey."

Carlyle considered this. "Excellent thinking, darling. There's a fair chance he'd have done it. So you're sure Mickey was behind the whole business?"

"Sure enough for your world," she said. "But not for mine. I don't have enough to arrest him."

"But it's plenty to remove him," Carlyle said. "All the same, you're right. We can't be swapping bullets with him and his people at present, no matter how much he deserves it. I'll speak with Corky and make sure he understands as well. The lad's been looking for an excuse to put a blade in Mickey for a while now."

"He's got the excuse if he wants it," Erin said grimly. "Mickey tried to kill me after the card game last night."

Carlyle's expression froze. "You were right to warn Ian off," he said quietly. "Never mind waiting. I'll take care of that gobshite myself, as soon as I'm up and about."

"I'm going to pretend you didn't say that," Erin said. "And no, you're not. You're out of your mind. He's ten years younger than you and twice your size, and you're no good with a gun. He'd kill you."

"I'll not go toe to toe with him," Carlyle said, still speaking in a low voice, but without a hint of softness. "I'm not mad. He'll simply climb into his car one of these days, turn the key, and get the biggest surprise of his life."

Erin put a hand over his. "Don't," she said. "I'm not having anyone commit murder for my sake."

"This isn't murder. It's defense, and it's necessary."

"Preemptive self-defense *is* murder. We'll get him," she promised the third man that day. "Just not yet. Think of it as an extra incentive to pull this off."

"It'd be simpler to get rid of him. But you're right, darling. If I'm to be walking the straight and narrow, I'd best get accustomed to it." He sighed. "Now, as to the meeting last night. Did Evan buy our bill of goods?"

"He bought it," she said, smiling grimly. "I'm in."

"Grand. Mickey knows you're lying, which is doubtless why he's out to get you."

"He's never trusted me and always hated me."

"You're a strong, confident woman and a police officer. Of course he hates you. He hates anyone he can't frighten or control, particularly lasses."

"Where do we go from here?" she asked.

"As soon as I'm out of this damned hospital, I'll be putting together information on the organization," he said. "I'm certain I'll be wearing recording devices at times. I know how these things go. And I'll collect documents, financial records, that manner of thing. Meanwhile, you'll be my trusty attack dog. It shouldn't take too terribly long, though that depends on a number of factors. For one, I'm not entirely certain where Evan keeps his own books. If we can find those, we'll have him cold. But one way or another, we'll win in the end."

"How are you feeling about it?"

He made a wry face. "I'm not accustomed to betraying people."

"You told me yourself they never trusted you," she pointed out. "It's hard to betray a trust that doesn't exist."

He gave her a startled smile. "Darling, you could have been the Devil's own lawyer, if you'd a mind that way."

"There's one other thing," she said.

"Aye? What's that?"

"My case agent agreed I need a safer place to sleep, after what happened with Siobhan and last night with Mickey. My apartment's no good, and I can't keep putting my brother's family in danger."

"I'm of the same opinion," he said. "You've a place in mind, I take it?"

"Yeah." She took a deep breath. "I was thinking maybe the Barley Corner would be a nice place to stay. For a while."

Carlyle looked at her for a moment, trying to read her.

"Aye," he said. "That'll be grand, I'm thinking. But I'm wondering what your da will say."

"He knows about us."

He blinked. "You neglected to mention that detail."

"Sorry. It slipped my mind, what with former prizefighters trying to crack my skull in and everything."

"If he's left even a mark on you..." Carlyle began.

"Stop it. You said I'm strong and confident just a minute ago. You don't need to protect me."

"Fair play, darling. But I'd hardly be any kind of a man if that miserable shitehawk didn't leave me right scunnered."

Erin snickered. "Your Irish comes out when you're angry."

"Ireland's whole history is a long list of old grudges," he said. "We've had plenty of practice being angry. I could say it in Gaelic if you'd rather."

"Then I'd have even less idea what you're saying."

"Have it your way, darling. I'll leave Mickey be. But I'm telling you now, he'll be more than a passing problem."

"We've handled worse."

He nodded, but didn't look completely convinced.

"Anyway," she added, "it'll be the two of us together. We'll be okay."

"As long as your da doesn't kill me."

"He won't. He just worries about me."

"On my account? Erin, I'm the only lad in the Life he needn't be worrying about!"

"What about Corky?"

"Particularly Corky."

Erin laughed. "Okay, good point." Then she stopped laughing. "I'm letting a murderer get away."

"Only for the moment. Your lads often leave one alone so he'll lead them to others."

"Yeah. But it doesn't feel right. My handler wanted to pull me out of the case, by the way. I told him I was in it to the end."

"Then we'll see it through," Carlyle said. "Together."

She reached for his hand. He took it and smiled at her.

Erin was living a double life, trying to balance right on the edge of disaster. On one hand was Evan O'Malley, Mickey Connor, and the rest of the Irish Mob. On the other was Lieutenant Keane and the NYPD. She was getting wrapped tighter and tighter in a web of obligations and expectations. Perception, as Carlyle and Finnegan had both said, was more important than reality, but Erin just hoped she could keep the one separate from the other. Almost everything might be a fake-out, a high-stakes gamble, but some things weren't. She had solid people she could count on: Carlyle, Phil Stachowski, Ian, Vic, Webb, even Corky. And Rolf, of course. Always Rolf. She wasn't alone.

She hoped that would be enough. Because things were going to get a whole lot worse before this was over, and she'd need all the help she could get.

"We'll see it through," she echoed.

Here's a sneak peek from Book 12: Aquarium

Coming 6/28/21

"All right, you sorry lot of scunners. Shut your mouths and open your ears. I've something to say."

All eyes turned to James Corcoran, "Corky" to his friends. He stood on top of the bar at the Barley Corner pub, his curly red hair nearly brushing the ceiling, a glass of Glen D whiskey in his hand and a smile on his lips. Conversation quieted to a murmur, then died away into silence.

"As all of you know, our friend and proprietor, Cars Carlyle, has had a few troubles of late. He's been a guest of New York's finest while recuperating from a very unfortunate injury. He's only just escaped from the hospital, and fortunately, the coppers didn't think it worth their while to pursue him. However, I do see they've a representative here among us today. But don't let that worry you, lads, she's one of us. You all know her. Stand up, Erin, love. Let the lads have a look at that stunner of a face."

Detective Erin O'Reilly stood up and waved good-naturedly to the crowd of Irishmen. Her wave was answered by a loud cheer and a few appreciative wolf-whistles. But it was all in good fun. The faces she saw around her were friendly. Even if they hadn't been, she wouldn't have been worried. She was carrying two guns, one at her hip, the other in an ankle clip, and her partner sat right beside her, scanning the crowd for any sign of trouble. She might be at a party, but Rolf was on duty. He had keen eyes, great instincts, unbelievable reflexes, and the best nose in the NYPD. The German Shepherd was ninety pounds of well-trained law-enforcement muscle and teeth, and he always had Erin's back.

"It's my understanding this lovely colleen saved my mate's life," Corky went on, drawing another cheer. "So it's only proper she's here for the lad's homecoming. Cars, lad, I don't know what you did to her that she fell for you instead of me. Think on it, lads. Look at my face, then look at his. I love him like a brother, but there's simply no comparison."

More laughter filled the room. On the other side of Erin from Rolf, Morton Carlyle just smiled and shook his head. In truth, he was at least as good-looking as Corky, a tall, silver-haired Irishman, impeccably dressed in a charcoal-gray suit and silk tie. He seemed perfectly healthy, his back straight as he sat on his customary bar stool. But Erin was close enough to see he still looked a little pale. A thin sheen of sweat was on his forehead.

She put out a hand and touched his arm. He met her eye and gave a very slight shake of his head, indicating he was fine for the moment. It was important not to show weakness, not in front of these men. All of them were affiliated with Evan O'Malley's mob, most of them under Carlyle's own command.

"It's all right, lad," Corky was saying. "I forgive you for recovering and keeping me from comforting this poor, brokenhearted lass. And I want to welcome you, on behalf of all of us, back to your proper place. Had you died, I'd have drunk a toast hoping you'd made it to Heaven a full half-hour before the Devil heard you were dead, but you lucky bastard, you're still breathing. So instead, I'll make a different toast. May we all be alive at the same time next year."

Several dozen hands hoisted glasses. Erin raised her own, a glass of Carlyle's best top-shelf whiskey. It was a little early in the day for drinking, but when a cop had to fit in, what could she do?

"Oh, and here's me forgetting," Corky said, pausing with his glass halfway to his lips. "Poor Cars here was hurt in the liver, the very worst place for an Irishman. So we're in this fine public house, drinking his fine liquor, and he can't be partaking. Well, I'm a lad who knows his duty, so I'll take it upon myself to drink for him."

He immediately put his money where his mouth was, downing his own drink in a single gulp, then dropping nimbly off the bar, snatching Carlyle's glass up, and swallowing another shot. Carlyle patted Corky on the arm with an affectionate smile. The two men shook hands and bent in close for a one-armed hug, Corky taking care not to touch Carlyle's wounded abdomen. There was another enthusiastic cheer.

Carlyle slowly, carefully got to his feet. He raised a hand. Silence descended again.

"Thank you, lads, for coming to welcome me home," he said. "It's grand to be back. Drink up, have a grand time. And don't forget to tip your waitresses. It's a hard job they have, putting up with you sorry lot."

Amid another burst of laughter, he sat back down, wincing slightly. Erin took hold of his arm more firmly.

"You need to lie down," she said quietly.

"Aye, that's a fine plan," he whispered back. "Now that I've put in an appearance, we can be fading into the background. If you'd be so kind?"

Erin offered her arm. He took it, keeping up the pretense that he was assisting her instead of the other way around. Perception was everything in this world. Carlyle had to look strong. She had to look dependent on him. Both of them had to look like firm supporters of Evan O'Malley. Corky had helped with his "one of us" comment, which hadn't been an accident.

All of it was a lie. Carlyle had been released from Bellevue Hospital after eight days of recovery from the nasty gut shot he'd received in Erin's apartment. He was better than he had been, but nowhere near full strength. He was relying on Erin right now. And neither of them was on Evan O'Malley's side. Carlyle was a week into his new job, which was that of turncoat and informant. Corky was in on the secret, and though he wasn't happy about it, he'd supported them so far.

"Everybody's watching," Erin said in an undertone as they steered toward the door at the back of the room. Rolf trotted at Erin's side, ears perked, alert.

"Of course they are," he said, smiling pleasantly and shaking hands with several guys they passed. "It's just like being a politician, darling. Everyone's watching you, all the time. Some people enjoy that sort of thing."

"They're crazy," she said, keeping a bright, artificial smile plastered on her own face as she said it. "It's like living in a damn goldfish bowl."

"If you're a goldfish, that's a fine place to live," Carlyle replied.

"As long as there isn't a cat around," she said. "Did you see Mickey?"

"I noticed him, aye. Near the doorway, surrounded by his bully-boys. He didn't seem as pleased with my recovery as some of the lads."

Neither of them said why Mickey Connor was unhappy, but both of them were thinking it. They were convinced Mickey had orchestrated the attempt on their lives that had left Carlyle in the hospital. Mickey was Evan O'Malley's chief enforcer, a retired heavyweight boxer with a disturbing affinity for violence and a strong dislike of both of them.

"Are you all moved in?" Carlyle asked, unlocking his door and ushering Erin through.

"Yeah, I brought the last stuff over last night," she said. "I left some things in storage, and some others with my brother, but I'm all moved out of my apartment. It's a little weird, staying here."

"Safest place you could be," he said. He took the stairs slowly and carefully. His abdominal muscles were still mending.

"Doesn't feel that way," she said. "There's four dozen armed thugs out there right now, getting plastered. Doesn't matter that it's nine in the morning, they're down there getting drunk like it's midnight."

"Ah, but they're my armed thugs."

"They're Evan's," she corrected him.

"Not all of them."

"Enough of them. If they knew what we were doing..."

"But they don't."

Erin nodded, hoping he was right. If he was wrong, the first warning was likely to be someone taking a shot at one of them. But right now, she was just glad he was out of the hospital and on the mend. It was a sunny morning in May, the air was warm, and it was good to be alive.

She turned at the top of the stairs, looped her arms around him, and kissed him lightly on the lips. "It's grand to be home, isn't it?" she asked, deliberately using one of his favorite words.

"Aye," he said. "And give me a few days, I'll be back in fighting trim. For now, though, I fear I'm needing a bit of a lie-down."

"Sure," she said. "Anything I can get for you?"

He shook his head and started to say something, but was interrupted by her phone. Erin pulled it out and saw Lieutenant Webb's name on the screen.

"I better take this," she said. She'd arranged her schedule so she wasn't supposed to be at the precinct for another half hour. Something must have happened.

"O'Reilly," she said, swiping the screen.

"We've got a body," Webb said by way of greeting. "Downtown hotel. The InterContinental on East 48th, in Midtown."

"I'm on my way," she said. Hanging up, she gave Carlyle an apologetic smile.

"Go on, darling," he said. "I promise not to do anything exciting while you're away."

"I think we've had enough excitement for a while," she said. "Just be alive when I get back."

"You worry too much, darling. I'm the picture of health."

"I was thinking about the goons downstairs."

"And I told you, they're my lads. Take care of yourself."

"I'll be fine. It's the other guy you should worry about."

*   *   *

"This is definitely out of our price range," Erin told Rolf as they got out of her Charger and walked up to the front of the InterContinental Hotel in Midtown.

Rolf wagged his tail. He wasn't bothered by economic concerns.

"And they wouldn't let you stay here," she added. "You're too big. Good thing you're with me."

He kept wagging. Being with his partner was definitely a good thing. Maybe the best thing.

She hurried up the steps to the front door. She didn't see any sign of the police. Whatever had happened, it hadn't required a large uniformed presence.

In the lobby, she caught sight of a familiar trench coat and fedora. Under the hat, talking to a couple of hotel employees, was Harry Webb, Erin's commanding officer. Next to him loomed Vic Neshenko, the other detective on Erin's squad. Vic was watching the room and chewing a toothpick that was wedged in a corner of his mouth. He saw Erin as soon as she entered and nodded curtly to her.

Erin and Rolf joined the group. The hotel workers looked like a manager and a housekeeper. The maid was a young, pretty Latina. She was obviously upset. The manager had a hand on her shoulder in what Erin hoped was a fatherly, comforting gesture.

Erin offered her hand. "Detective O'Reilly," she said.

The manager took his hand off the woman and shook. "Nicholas Feldspar," he said. "Floor manager. This is Rosa Hernandez."

"Where did this happen?" Webb asked Rosa.

"The Ballroom," the young woman said. "The Grand Ballroom, that is. Not the Empire."

"You've got more than one ballroom," Vic said in a flat, deadpan voice.

"On the mezzanine level," Feldspar put in. "We can go up those stairs." He pointed over his shoulder to an open staircase.

"Do I have to?" the woman asked. "It was so awful."

"I'm afraid so, Rosa," the manager said gently. "These people need our help."

"It'll be helpful if you can tell us exactly what you saw," Webb said.

"Nobody's in the room now, are they?" Vic asked.

"One of your officers is up there," Feldspar said.

"Good," Webb said. "Let's go."

"Glad you could join us," Vic said to Erin as they followed Feldspar to the stairs.

"How long have you guys been here?" she asked.

"Just got here," he said. "We don't know much. Apparently our girl was doing some cleaning in the public spaces. Y'know, since it isn't checkout time yet, she can't do the rooms. Anyway, she found a floater."

"A floater?" Erin echoed, not sure she'd heard him right.

He shrugged. "That's what she said."

"Vic, we're not on the waterfront. In the swimming pool maybe?"

"Maybe. But she said ballroom." He shrugged again. "I just hope we catch a beautiful woman this time, for a change of pace. I'm sick of dealing with ugly thugs."

They got to the top of the stairs. The manager led the way to the ballroom. Sure enough, a uniformed cop was standing outside the entrance, hands clasped at his belt buckle. Webb showed his gold shield and the uniform got out of the way.

The ballroom was as large and fancy as Erin expected, well-furnished and expensive. The south wall was what drew her attention. The hotel had replaced that whole wall with glass, behind which was a massive aquarium, lit from beneath with a soft blue glow. Tropical fish drifted in place or darted around in flashes of bright, dramatic color. In the middle of the aquarium, arms outstretched, hair floating out in all directions, a woman hung suspended in the water. A diaphanous dress billowed around her. In the blue light her skin looked pale and unearthly, like a porcelain doll. She might have been asleep, but her eyes were open and staring right at the detectives.

"Jesus," Vic muttered. "That's creepy."

"You said you wanted to catch a beautiful woman," Erin said very quietly.

"Not what I meant," he said.

Ready for more?

Join Steven Henry's author email list
for the latest on new releases, upcoming books and
series, behind-the-scenes details, events, and more.

Be the first to know about the release of Book 2 in
the Erin O'Reilly Mysteries by signing up at
tinyurl.com/StevenHenryEmail

About the Author

Steven Henry learned how to read almost before he learned how to walk. Ever since he began reading stories, he wanted to put his own on the page. He lives a very quiet and ordinary life in Minnesota with his wife and dog.

Also by Steven Henry

Ember of Dreams
The Clarion Chronicles, Book One

When magic awakens a long-forgotten folk, a noble lady, a young apprentice, and a solitary blacksmith band together to prevent war and seek understanding between humans and elves.

Lady Kristyn Tremayne – An otherwise unremarkable young lady's open heart and inquisitive mind reveal a hidden world of magic.

Robert Blackford – A humble harp maker's apprentice dreams of being a hero.

Master Gabriel Zane – A master blacksmith's pursuit of perfection leads him to craft an enchanted sword, drawing him out of his isolation and far from his cozy home.

Lord Luthor Carnarvon – A lonely nobleman with a dark past has won the heart of Kristyn's mother, but at what cost?

Readers love *Ember of Dreams*

"*The more I got to know the characters, the more I liked them. The female lead in particular is a treat to accompany on her journey from ordinary to extraordinary.*"

"*The author's deep understanding of his protagonists' motivations and keen eye for psychological detail make Robert and his companions a likable and memorable cast.*"

Learn more at tinyurl.com/emberofdreams.

More great titles from Clickworks Press

www.clickworkspress.com

Hubris Towers: The Complete First Season
Ben Y. Faroe & Bill Hoard

Comedy of manners meets comedy of errors in a new series for fans of Fawlty Towers and P. G. Wodehouse.

"So funny and endearing"

"Had me laughing so hard that I had to put it down to catch my breath"

"Astoundingly, outrageously funny!"

Learn more at clickworkspress.com/hts01.

The Dream World Collective
Ben Y. Faroe

Five friends quit their jobs to chase what they love. Rent looms. Hilarity ensues.

"If you like interesting personalities, hidden depths... and hilarious dialog, this is the book for you."

"a fun, inspiring read—perfect for a sunny summer day."

"a heartwarming, feel-good story"

Learn more at clickworkspress.com/dwc.

Death's Dream Kingdom
Gabriel Blanchard

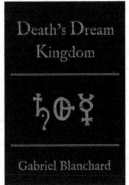

A young woman of Victorian London has been transformed into a vampire. Can she survive the world of the immortal dead— or perhaps, escape it?

"The wit and humor are as Victorian as the setting... a winsomely vulnerable and tremendously crafted work of art."

"A dramatic, engaging novel which explores themes of death, love, damnation, and redemption."

Learn more at clickworkspress.com/ddk.

Share the love!

Join our microlending team at
kiva.org/team/clickworkspress.

Keep in touch!

Join the Clickworks Press email list
and get freebies, production updates, special deals,
behind-the-scenes sneak peeks, and more.

Sign up today at clickworkspress.com/join.

CPSIA information can be obtained
at www.ICGtesting.com
Printed in the USA
BVHW090556300421
606130BV00012B/1463/J